BRODEN

Immortal Highlander, Clan Mag Raith Book 4

HAZEL HUNTER

HH ONLINE

Hazel loves hearing from readers!
You can contact her at the links below.

Website: hazelhunter.com

Facebook:
business.facebook.com/HazelHunterAuthor

Newsletter: HazelHunter.com/news

I send newsletters with details on new releases, special offers, and other bits of news related to my writing. You can sign up here!

Chapter One

STANDING IN THE shadows of Dun Chaill's great hall, Broden mag Raith watched Mariena Douet sleep. Firelight painted her with glowing colors, tinting the porcelain paleness of her hair and skin. Even from where he stood, he could smell the rain-washed headiness of her scent, like that of angelica after a storm. Absent expression, her face appeared calm, almost serene, yet her hands remained in loose fists. Blood flecked some of her fingers and stained the inside of one thin wrist.

Gazing upon her yet felt as if Broden had somehow gone mad.

For weeks he'd dreamt of this female, in both tantalizing detail and frustrating uncertainty. In hours of slumber he'd held and kissed and caressed her, giving and taking pleasures with her that only the most ardent lovers shared. For all the females he'd lain with over his long life, he'd never known such a consuming passion. He would have happily spent eternity in her arms, feasting on her as a sumptuous, unending banquet. Each time he awoke he was addled, almost convinced she could not be flesh.

Tonight, she'd dropped from the sky in the aftermath of a battle between his clan and the demonic Sluath, as if a victory boon from the Gods—an illusion that had lasted until the moment the lady had awakened.

In Broden's dreams he'd looked upon Mariena as if through eyes filled with rain, so that she seemed only a blur of pale hair and skin. Now he could see everything of her, from a tousled mane of white and light gold to the thin, arched elegance of her bare feet. Since she had arrived naked after escaping the demons, nothing of her provided a hint of what time she had been taken from by the Sluath. Her features, more handsome than pretty, appeared as young and innocent as any maiden's.

Her quickness and surety an hour past had banished that notion as well.

Edane, the clan's shaman-trained archer, finished his examination of the unconscious lady. He covered her with a wool blanket, taking care to cover her bare feet. He then scrubbed a hand over his long scarlet hair as he beheld her another moment.

"No wounds or bruising, thank the Gods," he told Domnall, the Mag Raith clan's chieftain. "'Tis likely she'll wake calmer once she's rested. Only dinnae be fooled by her look of frailty. That swan's skin covers muscles as fit and hard as a man's."

"Aye, and she fights as one." The big man regarded his mate. "This French tongue the lady first spoke, 'tis common in your time, Wife?"

"In France, Canada, and most of Europe, but not in my country." Jenna Cameron had come to the clan in fourteenth-century Scotland, but had been abducted from twenty-first century America, where she had worked as an architect. "Miss Douet used English with some fluency, and Rosealise speaks French like a native, so we shouldn't have any problem communicating with her."

No one mentioned the other reason they might expect difficulty with Mariena. Broden wondered if they thought it a kindness to him. He said nothing, aware as always that while his looks had always been called god-like, the sound of his harsh, damaged voice rasped unpleasantly in everyone's ears.

"One more thing," Jenna said, touching the chieftain's arm. "Her face looks familiar to me. I'm pretty sure that she escaped the underworld with the rest of us."

Domnall glanced at Broden, a flicker of sympathy in his green eyes before he said to his wife, "You should change into something dry, my love."

"We both need a bath first." The slender, dark-haired architect glanced down at her mud-spattered garments. "Before I hit the showers, I'll check on Nellie and Rosealise. They were both pretty shaken up by, ah, mademoiselle's introduction." She gave Broden a rueful look before she left the hall.

All gentleness left Domnall's expression as he regarded the two men. "You and Edane secure the hall so the lady cannae set fires or run loose. Mael has the keepe watch until dawn, and I the next. Kiaran isnae in any shape to relieve us, so sleep while you may." He headed after his wife.

Moving heavy stones to block the doorways provided welcome occupation for Broden, even with the odd weakness that had beset him since the battle. He then watched from the kitchens as Edane cast protective spells over the hearths and torches. When the archer stepped through to join him, he shifted the last blocks into place, effectively turning the hall into a spacious prison.

Through a gap in the stones he peered in at Mariena, only to assure himself that she still slept. When he turned around, he saw Edane bring out his box of medicines.

"I thought Kiaran but left muddled by the spell blast," Broden said, disuse rendering his voice little more than a grinder of words.

"'Tis no' for the falconer," the archer said, nodding toward his throat. "You yet bleed."

Touching the new wound atop the old scar on his throat, Broden took away his fingers to find them spotted with thick, dark blood. Until this moment there'd been no pain, but now it throbbed like a sore tooth. His hand also shook slightly, and he looked up to see Edane watching the tremor.

"Dinnae be a facking wench," Broden told him flatly. "'Tis naught but weariness."

The archer nodded, and with silent speed attended to the deep cut, cleaning it before he applied a soothing salve. As he did Broden stared past him without seeing anything but Mariena's face. It seemed now permanently fixed in his mind.

"'Tis better." Edane stepped back. "'Twill want a bandage if 'tis still open in the morning." His blue eyes shifted to Broden's, and filled with doubt. "I should see how Kiaran fares before I seek my lady and our bed." He hesitated before he touched Broden's shoulder. "Dinnae brood longer, Brother. I vow we'll fathom more on the morrow."

Broden doubted that, and everything else now, but Edane would not leave him if he thought him addlepated. "My thanks, and fair night."

Once the archer left, Broden retrieved a bottle of whiskey from their stores and drank directly from it. Although as an immortal he could no longer become drunk, the burn of the spirit distracted him from the throb of his neck.

It did nothing to soothe the churn of his thoughts.

Handsome as he surely was, Broden had fared none too well with females. His own mother, a headman's bed slave, had died bearing him. Sileas, his sire's vengeful wife, had then tried to strangle the life from him, forcing her mate to foster Broden with another tribe. There, among the Mag Raith, the one Pritani lass he might have loved had been openly humiliated for opening her heart to a worthless slaveborn like him. The *dru-widess* lovers he'd since taken had offered their bodies, never their affections.

Since she had begun appearing in his dreams his pale-haired lover had slowly become his one hope of happiness. She'd given herself to him again and again, holding nothing back, so generous and passionate a lover that he'd been humbled. She'd whispered her love to him as well, her voice sweet and low as she'd lavished him with affection and devotion. Surely if she had given her heart to him so entirely when they'd been slaves in the Sluath underworld, then it would be so again when she found him. At long last he would have a mate of his own, a woman with whom he could share his life and his heart.

So she had come, too, as suddenly as the battle with the Sluath had ended.

Seeing her fall from the sky had near paralyzed Broden. She'd been so still at first, he'd thought her dead, and he vaguely remembered falling to his knees in despair. Yet the Gods had not been so cruel as that. When he'd touched her, he'd felt her warmth and the whispering pulse of her heart. He stroked his hand over her hair, feeling again the slippery weight of it. In his dreams the its pale silk had veiled them as she'd kissed his throat and spoken of her love.

Her love indeed.

Upon awakening Mariena Douet had taken Broden's dagger and held it to his neck, pressing the blade deep to show the clan she was all too ready to cut his throat.

Broden emptied half the bottle before he set the whiskey aside and pressed his hand to his throat. Why the wound had not closed should have worried him. Thanks to the healing powers of his immortality he and the other Mag Raith hadn't suffered from a lasting injury in more than a thousand years.

From this ye cannae flee, Sileas's icy voice gloated from his memories.

THE MOMENT she opened her eyes Mariena knew

she had not returned to the Sluath underworld. She could put no name to this place and its weathered stone walls, vaulted ceilings and enormous fireplaces, but nothing about it stank of demons. Wood and herbs scented the air that was warm against her face. Only the flames in the fireplace moved—and the fire there burned golden and orange, not blue-white.

Je me suis échappé.

She had escaped death, and now could carry out her mission. For a moment Mariena lay and simply let herself breathe, her hands clutching the soft wool covering her. The blanket was dry and clean and marvelously warm, sensations that seemed unfamiliar. She'd not felt this way since… a time she could not remember. Only disjointed flashes of a terrible place and pain, echoed in the emptiness within. Fear stirred her fragmented thoughts into greater chaos.

A soft yet steely feminine voice came out of that inner turmoil: *Calme-toi, mon cygne. You cannot do the work if you are afraid. Attend to your mission.*

The name and face of the woman who had said that remained lost to her, as well as the details of the mission. All had been swallowed by the tempest that had taken Mariena.

The storm.

She had fallen through the thunder-filled skies. Plummeting through the clouds, she'd looked down at the ground rushing up at her, and felt… relief? Had she wanted to die so quickly? All around her demons had darted, battling huge, brawny men on flying horses. And there beneath her, a red-haired man with a desperate face. In his arms she'd seen the small woman with three arrows protruding from her back. The last thought that had come to her before the impact and the terrible pain in her belly had been about the wounded woman.

Nellie lives.

Carefully Mariena moved her hands under the blankets, feeling a thin shift over her nakedness. She ran her hands over her arms, breasts, belly and thighs before she rolled to her side. Her back did not ache. Her feet did not throb. None of her bones had broken. When she touched her skull nothing but damp hair and scalp slid under her fingers.

Healed.

Glancing around the room again, Mariena sat up and pushed the blanket away. Beneath it she found an amber and brown tartan that smelled of something that sent a rush of heat flashing through her. She'd taken it from a man with a face so handsome she'd assumed him to be Sluath. With those impossibly stunning features, how could he not be? He had radiated such unearthly perfection he surely could never have been mortal.

Taking his dagger had been a desperate attempt to defend herself from him.

Mariena lifted the tartan to her nose, breathing in deeply the mossy musk of him. Disarming him had been ridiculously easy, and in the next moment she'd smelled that same scent. That had assured her that he was not a demon. Whoever the man was, he'd likely had little fighting experience. No one had uttered his name, but no doubt it was something magnificent, to match that face and body. She did not blame herself for reacting as she had. Dazed from the fall, and terrified to find herself surrounded by strange faces, her first thought had been to protect herself.

Yes, with that glorious body of his.

Her move had been extremely foolish as well. If he'd been one of the demons, he would have simply snapped her arm in two. But no, for all his bewitching beauty he'd been all but helpless. Once she'd made sure there were no others waiting ready to pounce on her, she'd wrenched the plaid from his broad shoulder to cover herself. Yet shoving him away had made her feel even more naked.

Better that than wailing and throwing myself into his arms.

The other men and the women in this place had not attacked her. The tall Englishwoman who had spoken to her in French had promised they were friends who would do her no harm. The kindness in her dove-gray eyes had seemed genuine. Had she been the one to call her a swan and tell her to calm herself? Mariena reached for the memory of the voice again, but another came from the shadows, cold and yet somehow amused.

The demon's face suddenly thrust into her mind, first a melting blob that shimmered and reshaped itself into a mirror of her own features.

Have you ever seen a man whipped to death? Wouldn't you like to?

Pain shattered the memory, and Mariena stifled her cry of reaction with the tartan. She pushed herself off the pallet and hurried to the nearest doorway, stopping when she saw the stones that blocked it. They didn't budge, even when she shoved at them with all her strength. As she turned about, she saw more stones positioned in the same fashion, blocking every exit from the hall. All of them proved too heavy for her to move.

Such friends that they make me their prisoner.

But as quickly as the thought rose, Mariena pushed it away. She understood exactly why they had barricaded her in the hall. She'd cut one of their men, and promised to do the same to anyone who tried to touch her. She should feel lucky only to be confined. They might have put her in chains, or even killed her, and then her mission would be ruined.

Her mission…

If the rebels are to survive, they will need your power, the chilling voice of a different demon whispered from the darkness in her head. *That is why I send you forward, apart from the others, with these memories intact.*

Mariena gazed down at her shaking hands and touched her belly as more came out of the murkiness.

A traitor among the Sluath had helped her and the others to escape. There had been five

Scotsmen, all from an ancient era, and three other women who like her had been stolen from different times. The Scotsmen had been their lovers and protectors during their enslavement in the underworld, and had called themselves by one name: the Mag Raith.

Each of them had leapt into the stream of clouds beneath a bridge that crossed a storm-darkened sky, so they might come together in another time and place—not only to be free, but to find that which would defeat the Sluath. The traitorous demon had sent them here.

Mariena glanced around the barricaded hall. This was Dun Chaill.

You will be changed by this.

The power she acquired after she'd fallen from the sky allowed her to heal others by transference, or so the demon had claimed. Mariena had not quite believed it, but now knew it to be true. When she had dropped onto the dying woman—*Nellie Quinn, slave of the Sluath for almost a century*—Mariena had absorbed the wounds from her back into her belly, and saved the other woman's life. The pain of acquiring her wounds, however, had hurt just as much as if she'd been the one to take three arrows in the back.

She'd come close to dying. Was that her mission, to give her life so that another might live?

Mariena touched the glyphs etched over her shoulder and heart. The demon had altered her somehow, to give her this power. The same had been done to the other women. Only Mariena knew that it would allow them to remain with the Scotsmen, but only if everything went according to the traitor's plan.

You must tell no one.

Stepping back from the blocked door, Mariena surveyed the walls and ceiling, making note of the height of the narrow slit in the stones. She reached up a hand and stood on her toes. Cool air flowed from the opening, so it had not been blocked off. She then eyed the trestle table, and imagined it tipped on its end.

It should be just tall enough for her to reach that very slender window.

Chapter Two

FEELING THE CHILL of dawn creeping into the cottage, Galan Aedth tossed another log on the fire. While he prepared his morning meal, he knew it would only nourish his mortal body. The hunger that gnawed beneath his breastbone had become that which no hot brew or porridge would ever again assuage. Now he understood why the Sluath chafed at not being able to return to their underworld. All of them had grown starved for the myriad wicked delights awaiting them there.

Delights that he, too, would soon know, courtesy of Iolar. The Sluath prince had put the fulfillment of Galan's dreams within his grasp—in exchange for his service.

The burly form of a lowland farmer came

trudging into Galan's front room, his ham-size fists locked around the scrawny throat of a purple-faced mortal female. Galan turned to his bubbling porridge and gave it a stir.

"This one I took on last night's raid is defective." The farmer tossed the wench at Galan's feet. "Our prince wishes you to repair her so she may attend his needs."

Galan glanced at the choking female, noting the thick, milky caste over her eyes. "Naught is broken. She's blind."

"What?" The farmer's body shifted into that of a towering highland warrior as Seabhag bent over to peer at the wench's mottled face. "How?"

Galan stifled a contemptuous laugh and instead took his morning brew from the hearth. Even the most novice of acolytes could have answered such a question. Though he'd shed his dreary life as a druid by leaving the Moss Dapple, he'd kept his knowledge.

"Sickness or injury," he told the Sluath. "Some bairns come from the womb thus." He reached down to send a flick of power through the woman, who went limp. "If Prince Iolar wishes to torment her, he must use something other than illusions." Galan took a sip of his bitter black tea. "She's four other working senses."

"That is too much work. I will put her in the barn to see to the horses." Seabhag eyed the steaming tea in Galan's hand. "Even now you must drink. How amusing. Do you still piss as well?"

Galan's grafted wings threatened to unfurl and he considered tossing the hot liquid in the demon's face, but instead he saw an opportunity.

Though Iolar had given him more power than he'd ever dreamed he'd command, the resurrection of his Pritani wife, Fiana, still remained tantalizingly out of reach. To bring his beloved back from the dead Galan had but to locate and capture Culvar, the demon-mortal halfling that the rest of the Sluath believed dead. Secretly discovering that the outcast still lived had not only restored his hope of being reunited with his wife, but also fulfilled his other desire: the ability to cheat death forever. Through Culvar, Galan would become like the Gods themselves, eternal and invincible. Immortality would also give him ample time to find and avenge himself on the Mag Raith, once his to command but now the most elusive of enemies.

"I piss like the Mag Raith did, I imagine, when you captured them. Where did you find them as mortals?"

Seabhag grunted as he crouched down, shifting his form into a duplicate of the blind maid. "Nowhere. They found their way to us through one of the portals." He glanced up at him. "It should have killed them. No mortals may pass through them."

Galan went still as he realized something he'd always assumed: the Mag Raith had come back to the mortal realm made immortal by the Sluath. Yet he himself knew that the process required much more than mere magical transformation. None of the hunters had been given wings or the sort of power Galan wielded. Just how had they managed to convince their captors to bestow on them the gift of eternal life?

"Doubtless they used Pritani magic to protect themselves from the portal," Galan replied. Now that he had confirmed his suspicions, he knew he had to go carefully. "More of such men came to the underworld in the past?"

Seabhag shook his head. "Now and then we'd find them in the midst of a cull, but..." He stopped and his eyes narrowed. "Why are you questioning me?"

"I merely wish to understand the process that I shall soon undergo." Galan lifted the wench's limp body, and covered her eyes with his hand. Murmuring under his breath, he removed the cataracts, clearing the irises. "There. When she awakes, she shall be especially terrified. I would give her to the prince now."

"And what do you want in return?" the demon demanded as he snatched the wench from him.

"Do you remember what portal the Mag Raith used to enter the underworld?" When Seabhag nodded, Galan casually sipped from his mug. "Tell me where I may find it."

"You already know. It's in the ridges near that miserable village you burned to the ground." The Sluath eyed him and then chuckled. "You can't use the damn thing, idiot. Aside from the fact it would kill you, it was sealed along with all the others. You saw that yourself when you tried to open it."

Galan hid a smile. "Indeed."

Chapter Three

STARS STILL GLINTED in the sky when Broden finally abandoned his luckless attempts to sleep and rose to dress in the darkness. Leaving the stronghold through the rebuilt tower arch allowed him to avoid the great hall as he went out to the stock barn. There he found the cows already standing in their stanchions, ready to be milked.

That was the way of it. Life went on, regardless of him.

"Fair morning, sir," Rosealise Dashlock said as she emerged from the storage room carrying just-washed buckets. A kerchief held back the unruly braids of her curly blonde hair, and she'd donned one of her voluminous aprons to protect her gown. "I used to milk our family cow, and after our grueling night I thought Nellie should like a sleep-in."

Broden tugged at the bandage across his throat, and wished Rosealise had done the same. "'Tis kind of you, my lady."

She halted and peered at him. "Egad, Broden, you look absolutely coopered. What is the matter? Should I fetch Edane?"

"No, my lady. As you say, 'twas a grueling night." He took the pails from her. "I'll see to the stock."

The housekeeper reached out to touch his arm, appeared to think better of it, and sighed. "When you're finished, dear sir, do come to the kitchens. I'll have a hot brew and fresh scones waiting."

Broden nodded, and took down his stool. Tending to the cows would take longer without Nellie, who had spent her girlhood on a dairy farm, but he didn't mind. The rhythm of the work lulled him, unraveling his thoughts from their snarls. Nothing could be done about his wretched bitterness. That had dogged him long before his awakening in the Moss Dapple's ash grove. That which he had hoped for had not come to pass. At Dun Chaill Mariena would be kept safe, and he'd seek contentment in that.

Unbidden, the last dream in which Broden had beheld his lover returned to him. Now he could see what before had remained a mystery: her handsome features, sun-dappled eyes, and the full lips she moved against his fingertips.

Gods, but she'd felt more dream than woman.

Her kisses had been so soft, like the whisper of silk over flesh. She'd not said a word, but crawled atop him, her body warm and pliant, her breasts pillowed on his chest as she'd bent her head to his. He'd worked his hands into all the pale, cool hair, then held her to look all over her face. Nothing had ever been, or would ever be, as lovely and rare and precious as her gold-shot blue eyes, filled with emotion. No one in his life had ever looked upon him with such love.

How could he have forgotten her? And Mariena, had she truly loved him? Or had Broden imagined it, riddled with envy and loneliness as he was over his brothers finding their mates so easily?

"You must show me how to attend to the milking," Domnall's deep voice said from behind him. The chieftain took the brimming pail from his grip. He cast a wary eye at the waiting heifers. "I should take a turn, but Nectan forbad me from such work."

"Your sire couldnae bend to it, for the stick of pride he kept tucked in his arse. But you neednae, for I've finished." Broden gave him a second bucket before retrieving two more and walking with him to the buttery. "'Twillnae do for you to play dairy maid, Chieftain. Your speed unsettles the stock."

"Ah, well." Domnall watched him filter the first bucket into a pan before he did the same. "Mistress Douet's soon to awake. I'd have you remove the stones, that we may speak and mayhap break our fast with her."

That wasn't all that Domnall wanted from him, Broden thought, and scowled. "Dinnae give her a blade with her food."

"I ken she's no' as you reckoned her, Brother," the chieftain said, grimacing, "but 'twill sort itself out with time. I've no doubt she's your lady."

"I facked her in my dreams," Broden corrected him. "Just as I took every *dru-widess* among the Moss Dapple willing to bed me, and more females from your tribe than you wish to ken. Dinnae frown at me. The whelp of a bed slave hasnae more to offer than such fleeting pleasures."

For a moment Domnall looked as if he might argue the point. Then he said, "You yet ken the lady better than the rest of us. Until her memories return she'll need to be watched, and somehow gentled. We cannot treat her as anything less than welcome. By my distrust and Kiaran's suspicions we nearly lost Nellie. I'll no' have another female thus driven from the clan."

"Nor I." Thinking of Mariena running away from Dun Chaill made Broden's gut knot. "What shall I do?"

"For now, show her you've no hard feelings over her attack on you." Domnall nodded toward the keepe. "Befriend her if you may. Yet until we're sure she's accepted us as friends, I dinnae want her to stray far beyond your sight."

"Oh, aye." Broden almost laughed out loud. "Mayhap you should shackle us together."

The chieftain grunted. "That I neednae do. You've given less attention to a wounded grice charging a blind."

Domnall didn't need to point out his ridiculous predicament. The fact that he'd been bewitched by a female he knew nothing about had to be obvious to everyone.

"I'll watch over her," Broden said.

Following Domnall into the stronghold yet called on all of Broden's nerve, for in truth he dreaded seeing the lady again. Yet when he shifted the stones aside, he saw the trestle table standing on end, and Mariena standing on the short ledge of the window slit, half her body through the narrow opening. If she meant to jump–

He dashed across the hall to put himself beneath her. "My lady, no."

Mariena slid back inside from the opening, frowned down at him, and then lowered a questing foot as she tried to reach the top end of the table. As soon as she planted her sole it tilted, and she lost her balance and fell.

Broden caught her in his arms, holding her too tightly for a long moment before he lowered her to the floor. A tingling warmth suffused him, and all he could do was look down at her, horrified and mesmerized. All of her loveliness, in his arms, against his body—it was as if he'd stepped into one of his dreams awake.

The Frenchwoman regarded him without expression. “You are quicker today.”

“You’re no’.” He wanted to stroke her back with his hands, but forced himself to release her. Try as he might, however, he could not step away. “I’m Broden.”

Wood scraped across stone as the leaning table fell over with a loud crash.

She didn’t even blink. “*Enchanté.*”

❧

BRODEN SEEMED AS ENTHRALLED as Mariena felt, which confused her. He should be angry over how she’d hurt and humiliated him last night. Her climb up to the window must have appeared to him that she was trying to escape. Should she explain she meant only to look outside and take in more of her surroundings? To see if anything about this place prompted her to remember why they’d been sent here? By doing so she might betray some details of her own mission…not that she could recall much of that.

Looking into his eyes seemed all she could do. She would find her tongue in a moment, as soon as this strange feverish heat faded. Why did she feel as if she might burst into flames just standing so close to the man? Did it come from him?

"I've no dagger for you this morning," he murmured.

"Your voice." Without thinking she reached for the wound she'd left on his neck. "You're scarred."

"Aye, my lady." He stiffened as she touched him there. "A gift from another who wished me dead."

Was that what he thought? "I don't want to kill you, *mon ange*." His eyes narrowed at the strange words. "I don't want to kill you, my angel. But if you have a spare blade, I will keep it safe for you."

"I dinnae wish to give you a blade," Broden muttered as she kept her fingers in place.

Heat flashed through her, streaming through her arm and into her hand. Beneath her light touch the cut on his neck began to shrink, and Mariena quickly stepped back. Since Broden did not react, he must have felt nothing. But as new pain burned across her own throat she turned and strode to the pallet to retrieve the tartan she'd taken from him.

Until I can control this power, I must not touch anyone else.

His people came into the hall, and their unhurried approach made her suspect they'd been watching her and Broden. She counted four: the tall, austere-looking chieftain, the bigger, massive seneschal, the tall, stately Englishwoman and the petite, dark-haired American. *Domnall, Mael, Rosealise and Jenna.* Recalling their names made her head feel as if it were filled with needles, but a moment later the pain faded. It seemed more of the demon's work, or perhaps part of the transference power.

The traitor did not want me to remember all.

She touched her throat to assure the wound had closed, and then draped herself with the tartan before she faced them. They appeared as uneasy as she felt, which proved a little reassuring. "*Bonjour.*"

Domnall looked from the overturned trestle table to her. "Fair morning, my lady."

"'Twas but a mishap," Broden told the chieftain.

"Pah. Don't lie for me. I'm to blame." Mariena studied the faces watching her, feeling her own wariness slowly receding. "None of you are French?"

The chieftain then performed introductions, confirming the names she had recalled, and identifying them as Scottish, English and American. "We welcome you to Dun Chaill, my lady."

"I am happy to be here, Monsieur." The one who seemed most familiar to Mariena was the pretty American with the curious eyes. To her she said, "You are the architect, no?"

"Yes, I'm Jenna Cameron." The chieftain's wife stepped forward, obviously fascinated. "You know me?"

"You and the others, yes." The only face she couldn't envision was the demon who had helped them flee. Then she understood. "Ah. You do not remember me." That made everything more complicated. She'd hoped someone else might be part of this mission of hers.

"I've seen your face," Jenna said slowly. "You were with us when we went to the sky bridge to escape. Other than that, well, we don't know much at all about you. The Sluath took away nearly all of our memories of the underworld and each other."

"The demons, they are pigs, no?" Mariena

regarded the others. "It is true that we escaped together, the nine of us. One of the Sluath, a traitor, sent us to come here, to meet at the castle, to find…something. That I cannot remember."

"Have you recalled anything about your past, or the time from which you were taken?" Rosealise asked, brushing back a wayward pale curl from her pretty face.

Mariena shook her head. "Those memories, they are gone." She turned to the chieftain. "Monsieur, last night, I was confused. Broden's face, it made me think him to be a demon. Now I see he is prettier than the demons. Forgive my *hostilité*."

Domnall smiled, transforming his stern features. "'Tis already forgotten, Mistress Douet."

A short time later Mariena sat down with the men and their ladies at the now slightly battered trestle table to share their morning meal. Rosealise apologized for the lack of coffee and tea as she poured a fragrant hot brew for her, explaining that neither had yet been introduced to Scotland in this time. Learning that she had dropped into the fourteenth century should have seemed beyond her understanding, but that, too, felt acceptable.

What the traitor wished them to find in a derelict castle like Dun Chaill remained an enigma, one that made her head ache whenever she thought on it. But why would the demon not let her remember that? Surely it had nothing to do with her mission.

Mariena sensed Broden paying close attention to her, and wondered if he would prove an obstacle. He might look like the dream of every woman, but his actions showed him to be clumsy and unwise. It had been far too easy for her to take his blade and use him as a hostage last night. Yet when she met his gaze for a moment, she felt that unwelcome heat stirring again inside her.

I cannot be distracted by him and his handsome face.

To feel marginally safe here Mariena would need a weapon. Jenna mentioned that the men carried swords because guns had not yet been invented in this time, which oddly comforted her. She would ask for a blade of iron like the one the chieftain carried in a sheath on his back. With that she could easily lop off a head, or cut open a demon from chin to belly, but even one thrust of iron into their bodies would poison them.

Her own thoughts gave her pause.

How do I know such things?

"Is there anything I can tell you about us or Dun Chaill?" the American asked.

More than she cared to inquire about, Mariena thought. "I remember another man who was injured, no?"

"That would be Kiaran." Jenna grimaced. "He's still, ah, recovering from the battle."

And no one wanted to talk about him, she could see that. She filed away their discomfort for later, and asked, "Where are we in Scotland, and why did we come here?"

"This is the eastern highlands. We're in the same place where our men were taken by the Sluath." The chieftain's wife described the region. "We came here hoping to find some answers about what happened to us. While the Mag Raith were in the underworld someone made this fortress into a castle, and then later abandoned it. There's also a spell boundary that protects us from the demons. We don't know who created it, but Edane believes the Sluath can't sense us when we're inside."

Complicated and mysterious—these were two of her least favorite things. "You went beyond the boundary last night."

The architect explained why they had chosen

to leave the safety of the castle to rescue their friend from the Sluath. Outnumbered as they were by the demons, it seemed to Mariena a preposterously foolish risk to take. Yet their loyalty to each other seemed stronger than their sense of self-preservation, and that made her like them even more.

Listening to Jenna tell the tales of the clan's adventures also gave Mariena time to eat. Their food, while simple, proved delicious. She devoured the berry-studded porridge as if she'd been starved, and drank two mugs of the housekeeper's fragrant flowery brew.

She also thought it interesting that Domnall allowed the women to inform her of what they had endured since escaping the underworld. He did not make it obvious, but he paid close attention to her, likely to gauge her reactions. She imagined little escaped the chieftain's watchful eyes.

"Since we arrived I've been working with the men to restore the castle, and make it more livable," Jenna said. "Rosealise has been kind enough to look after all of us as our housekeeper. Nellie's family had a farm, and she's very knowledgeable about the livestock, so I expect she'll take over as our dairy manager."

"The little one milks cows?" Mariena pressed her lips together as she nodded. "She is stronger than she looks."

"We've all, ah, special gifts," the architect said, giving her husband a rather pointed look. "They do come in handy."

What the American seemed too polite to ask, Mariena thought, was what *she* could do. Since her past remained lost to her, she could not volunteer any particular skill. Her hard thoughts and ease with weapons made her wonder if she even wished to remember the life the demons had stolen from her.

She smiled at Jenna. "I do not remember my life, but I am a woman. I probably kept house and cooked food and perhaps milked cows. I do not think I built castles, but you do that already. Anyway, I will help."

"You did swell just dropping in last night, doll," a wry voice said.

As a lanky, red-haired man and another petite woman entered the hall, Mariena felt a surge of satisfaction to see Nellie, and how she moved with ease. Perhaps Mariena had done terrible things in her past, but here she had saved a life. That felt very good.

"'Tis fortunate the stronghold brought you back to me, my lady," the man said to Nellie, and kissed her temple. "For I couldnae do without you." He smiled at Mariena. "I'm Edane mag Raith. I'm the clan's archer and shaman."

"Hello." They didn't know she had taken Nellie's wounds, Mariena thought, but why would Edane think the castle had revived her?

Again, the traitor's words whispered in her head. *You must tell no one.*

As Rosealise made to fill two more bowls for the couple, the archer shook his head.

"No' yet, my lady." He regarded Domnall. "We should go to the greenhouse now, Chieftain. All of us."

Chapter Four

IN THE WARREN of tunnels deep beneath Dun Chaill's great hall, amber torchlight flickered over Cul as he watched the Mag Raith and their females leave the stronghold. His misshapen body shuffled back and forth as he studied the new, pale-haired female they had brought back from their battle with the demons. Unlike the Pritani, he could sense her healing power, which explained how Nellie Quinn had been restored to life after dying in her lover's arms.

The little American had spent too much time in the underworld to survive the wounds. How perfect, then, the timing of the Frenchwoman's fall, as if Fate itself had foreseen the outcome of the battle.

Cul snorted. He didn't believe in Fate. Mariena Douet had been purposefully altered before escaping the Sluath underworld to save Nellie Quinn. But for what purpose? Surely the demon traitor would not care if the Mag Raith or their women lived or died.

I must learn more.

The secret system of mirrors and tubes he'd built to permit him to spy on every part of his castle had never been more vital to Cul. What he saw and heard dictated nearly all of his actions of late. He resented being made to scurry about and eradicate every trace of his spell work from the castle's upper levels. But Nellie Quinn would be much harder to kill now that she had been awakened to immortality, and he could not risk exposing his presence again. The Mag Raith might decide to set fire to his beloved Dun Chaill.

He had not worked for centuries and come this close to attaining his vengeance for it to slip through his grasp over a woman.

Cul hobbled along the passage that led to the new listening post he had placed in the greenhouse. Although Edane had bespelled the structure to prevent anything said within from being heard outside, he had not thought to extend the magic across the expanse of the dirt floor. It had been simple for Cul to dig from beneath and place a tube under one of the work tables.

"There used to be a gate to the underworld in that cave," he heard Nellie saying. "It was bespelled to kill mortals, so Galan had me touch-read the stone floor in front of it. The thing that built Dun Chaill—the monster—also sealed off that gate. From what I saw, I think it's part demon and part human, but it looks just like Prince Iolar."

"Did you tell Galan you had seen this thing here?" Domnall asked.

"No, Chief, I'm not that stupid," Nellie assured him. "All I did was describe the monster to him, and then he said something strange: 'Culvar lives.' He also said he'd cut out my tongue and slit my throat if I said anything about it to the demons."

So, the wicked druid had learned much, Cul thought, gripping the tube until the bronze began to crumple. Forcing himself to release it, he put his ear to the opening again.

"If the watcher that threatens your castle is

this Culvar, then he could be what the demon wished us to find," Mariena said. "He can perhaps do more than close off these gates."

That a mortal female thought with tactical perception surprised Cul, who had assumed such insight beyond a woman's experience and understanding. The newcomer might prove useful to him. But for now he had to attend to maintaining his own protection. With all the intruders outside the keep he could summon the last of his yet-hidden iron warriors to stand guard in the passages of his subterranean lair.

Cul limped back through the tunnels before he cast his summoning spell. He felt the muffled, metal footfalls more than he heard them, as his troops came to him from several tunnels. Each fell into a single line as they awaited his new commands. He posted pairs at each underground entrance. Drained and yet determined to make the most of the respite, Cul then went through the passages of the stronghold to neutralize the spells of the tracking stones Edane had scattered through the keepe.

Backtracking over his own steps, Cul cast another spell to erase every trace of his presence before descending beneath the castle. As he did, pain lanced through his crippled leg, now rendered almost useless from newly-healed breaks. The bones, which had already been distorted, had fused together in a crazed jumble after being shattered in the tower collapse. His immortality could repair almost any injury, but thanks to his human blood it would never make him whole or hale.

In his sleeping chamber Cul dropped onto his pallet and regarded the lumpy ruin of his leg. Being held captive in the underworld for so long leeched the humanity out of the enslaved, until they either went mad or changed into Sluath. He'd sensed that Nellie had been very close to transitioning.

Rubbing a gnarled hand over his twisted limb, he imagined it straight and whole again, as it had been before his escape to the mortal realm. If Mariena could heal a mortal who was mostly demon, could she do the same to a halfling like him?

Before he could even consider using Mariena, he would have to first test the limits of her power. His mouth formed its sneer of a smile as an idea of how to go about that took shape. If it proved successful, he might regain his former freedom of movement. If it did not, then the most inconvenient of all the intruders would be quashed.

In this he could not lose.

Chapter Five

MIDSUMMER CLAD THE outer walls of Dun Chaill with buttery light in the early mornings, spangling the glints in the weathered ashlar as Broden made his way outside. Warm air scented with wildflowers and ripening grasses washed over him as he followed the trail of small footprints in the dew toward the forest. Nellie was teaching Edane how to milk and look after the herd, so Broden was not needed in the barn. Still, he should be checking his snares, and then casting hook lines while the waters teamed with the warm season's bountiful runs of salmon and trout.

So Broden would be attending to them now, had the canny wench not eluded him yet again.

Watching over Mariena as she adjusted to life

at Dun Chaill had proven a more difficult task than Broden had imagined. Unlike the other ladies who had joined the Mag Raith the Frenchwoman said very little and kept to herself. She seldom retired until after midnight, and usually rose before dawn. After they had prepared a chamber for her use, she asked they remove half the furnishings. She then shifted what remained into a curious arrangement around the door. He only realized why after several days, when he heard the sounds she made before emerging from the chamber. When she'd left, he looked in and saw the state of the blankets she'd piled in one corner.

"She sleeps on the floor," Broden later told Domnall and Mael. "The bed and wash stand she moves each night to barricade herself in the chamber."

"Likely the lass fears an intrusion," the big seneschal said. He didn't have to name the watcher. They all remained on their guard when speaking where they might be overheard. "I'll install a bolt bar within to ease her worry."

"If 'tis the true cause." The chieftain frowned at Broden. "What reckon you?"

He shrugged. Much about Mariena fashed

him, from her terse, enigmatic manner of speaking to the care and silence with which she moved. "Mayhap 'tis a common practice in her time."

"If so, then she's learned few others," Mael said. "She's ever willing to work, but hasnae ease nor skill with any household tasks. She burned most of the morning meal while Rosealise was out tending the garden, and mangled a skirt she attempted to mend for my lady. How cannae a female no' ken how to cook or sew?"""

"Jenna didnae when she came to us," Domnall pointed out. "Females lead very different lives in the centuries to come. I've no doubt Mistress Douet possesses other skills that with time we'll discover."

"She should be told now that we're immortal," Broden said abruptly, "and we've abilities beyond what we had before the Sluath took us." Before either man could argue he added, "We kept much from Nellie, and she in turn concealed her touch power from us. 'Tis better no' to make the same mistake again."

The chieftain nodded. "Jenna said much the same to me. We shall speak with her when we gather in the hall."

That night over the evening meal Mariena listened as Domnall revealed the truth about the clan's long lives. Their injuries always healed, though their immortality had never been put to the test with fatal wounds. Old age and disease were something they would never know. He described their remarkable abilities until he'd finished relating the last of their secrets. Jenna then told her how the castle had brought her, Rosealise and Nellie back to life and bestowed immortality on them.

Mariena took a sip from her mug of water. "Is this why you think your tattoos changed color?"

"We're not quite sure," Rosealise admitted, "although it seems to happen just after death, when our bodies were brought here. Whatever magic revives us, it also changes the color of our husbands' markings at the same time." She touched the golden glyph's on Mael's arm.

Edane kissed Nellie's hand and smiled. "I much prefer my ink, now that 'tisnae black." He glanced up as Kiaran quietly entered the hall. "'Tis good to see you join us for the meal, Brother."

"Rosealise made a medieval version of Mulligatawny soup," Nellie chimed in. "It's the bee's knees." She filled a bowl for him, and passed the bread platter.

The falconer murmured his thanks, nodded to Mariena as he took the food, but then carried it with him as he departed.

Throughout the remainder of the meal Broden watched Mariena's face, but she showed no reaction other than interest. Later the question she had asked came back into his mind, echoing as he tried but failed to fathom why it nagged at him. Perhaps it was the fact that she didn't speak perfect English, but nonetheless it stayed with him.

Is this why you think your tattoos changed color?

To keep his promise to Domnall and to satisfy his own curiosity about Mariena, Broden had taken to tracking her from a discreet distance wherever she went. This morning she'd left before the rest of the clan had risen, doubtless to again walk around the outer walls of the keepe. She did so twice before returning each day. Once inside the castle she said nothing of her walks, but would go directly to the kitchens to help Rosealise with the morning meal.

At first Broden assumed Mariena sought to look upon what lay beyond Dun Chaill, but she paid no particular attention to any of the woods, gardens or outbuildings beyond the keepe. Instead she looked as if she were surveying all of it for signs of something. Then the purpose of her walks came to him one night as he saw Kiaran leave to ride along the spell boundary.

Mariena didn't leave every morning to go walking or explore the grounds. She went on her own private patrol.

At the edge of the woods Broden halted as he saw the lady's footprints stray from her usual path into the woods between the stronghold and the river. His fists clenched as he peered into the trees, but he saw no sign of her. Nellie had taken the same path when she'd stolen a horse and escaped Dun Chaill, which in the end had led to her capture by Galan and the Sluath.

A tight anger seized him. With so many of her memories yet intact Mariena had to know how dangerous the demons were, and what they would do to her to learn where the Mag Raith had hidden. She'd put them all at risk by fleeing. Or did she mean to run from him? Had she at last recalled that they had been lovers?

If she had not, then by the Gods, as soon as

he found her he'd tell her. He'd waited long enough.

Broden ran into the woods, dodging branches and tearing through the thick bracken. Twigs and leaves pelted his tunic by the time he emerged in the clearing by the river. A shaft of light flooded his eyes before he saw her. The soft rush of the water filled his head like a distant rain storm while his heart pounded in his head. She hadn't run from him.

She hadn't run at all.

White-gold sunlight poured over Mariena, who stood knee-deep in the midst of the currents. Only a short, sodden shift clung to her pale body as she bent over. Streams of water poured from her sleek tresses, which she held in a twisted mass she was wringing. On the bank she'd left the gown and boots Jenna had given her, neatly stacked atop his tartan. The smell of lavender and roses came to him, and he looked until he spied a small crock in the grass. It contained the mild herbal soap Rosealise had rendered for herself and the other women.

The reason she'd altered her path and come to the river was to wash her hair.

Relief and fury warred inside Broden as he

strode down to the edge of the bank. Yet as soon as he drew nearer his steps slowed. Mariena's Sluath tattoo showed through the shift she wore, made almost transparent by the water. Along with the black glyphs it showed every curve of her body with adoring detail, from the lyre of her hips to the ripe perfection of her breasts.

The light bathed her as beautifully as the water. Droplets glistened on her arms, with smaller beads nestled against her lashes and cheeks and lips like so many tiny, scattered crystals. The washing had turned her hair from white-gold to a light honey color, and when she released it the strands unraveled to spill over her alabaster shoulders like gilded silk.

For a moment Broden wondered if he still lay in his chamber, asleep and dreaming. Never once in his long life had he beheld a sight lovelier than this.

Finally, he forced himself to clear his throat. "My lady?"

"There you are," Mariena said as she turned to regard him. Her brows arched over her gold-patched blue eyes as she took in his disheveled state. "You're slow to catch up this morning, *mon charmant*. Did I walk too fast?"

❧

SEEING the handsome Scotsman staring at her was nothing new, but Mariena had grown weary of his shadowing her. Domnall mag Raith had assured her the clan did not regard her as their prisoner. He'd also said that as long as she remained inside the spell boundary she could go wherever she wished. Yet from the day she'd fallen into his arms Broden had kept trailing after her, as if she could not be trusted. Occasionally, like this morning, she thought another member of the clan was doing the same.

Broden's brows drew together. "Why do you call me those words?"

"*Mon charmant?*" Startled, she hadn't realized she'd been addressing him in French. "In English it is like a charming one, what we called, ah…" She grimaced as a sharp pang stabbed into her head. "I cannot remember now."

"Dinnae try. Remembrance brings pain." He picked up the tartan she'd left on the bank and held it out to her.

"I'll ruin it, drenched as I am," she told him as she waded to the bank and climbed out of the water. Sitting down on the soft grass, she stretched out her legs and lifted her face. "The sun will dry me, and then I shall go back and help Rosealise, if she needs something burned. See to your rabbit traps."

Broden dropped the tartan beside her but did not leave. Instead he kept his face averted, and stared at the ridges.

Mariena squinted up at him. The morning lit his stunning face, adding a glow to all that perfection. She did not have to remember her life to know he was the most beautiful man she'd ever seen. No one in all of time had ever looked like Broden. The shining flow of his midnight hair seemed as polished as the dark diamonds of his eyes. His glorious skin might have been molded from some rare golden wood, and showed not a single wrinkle or blemish. His scent matched his allure, bold and yet unexpected. She admired the length of him, tall but not towering, and the shape of him, powerful yet not massive.

She tried not to imagine him naked. That made everything below her neck begin demanding she make him that way before she tore off her clothes.

Would Broden prove as magnificent a lover? She doubted it. For a man to look as marvelous as he did meant that he attracted the eyes of any woman. He had to do little more than smile to be lavished with fawning adoration. Like all such men he probably regarded it as his due. He likely had left a trail of broken-hearted lovers from here to France.

His expression seemed as remotely superb as ever, but the rigid set of his shoulders hinted at what he was feeling. Since he'd been following her, she had to be the cause.

"You are angry with me for coming here? Why? It is forbidden to be clean in this time?"

"I ken Jenna showed you the bathing chamber in the castle." He made a sharp gesture at the river. "Yet you come here, with no word to anyone. I reckoned you'd run from us. If you'd slipped and fallen, or…" He stopped and looked away. "'Tisnae safe."

"Pah. I fell from the sky into your battle with demons, and lived," she reminded him. "I think I may survive a dip in this little stream."

"Many mortals caught alone in these lands ended slaughtered." His jaw tightened. "We protect our ladies at Dun Chaill, Mistress."

Ah, so she'd offended him with her independent ways. Was that why he kept tag-tailing after her, out of some sense of misplaced gallantry? As fine as he was to look at, Mariena had no intention of allowing him to become her minder, not when she had to find her target. She could not remember her mission, but with her particular skills it seemed obvious: the demon had sent her here to kill someone. Since the traitor had helped these people, her target had to be the watcher.

"You are very gallant. I like this." She picked up the tartan and wrapped it around herself as she stood, but then stepped close enough to grip the hilt of his dagger. "But who protects you, *mon ami*?"

His hand covered hers with a grip too loose to stop her from taking the blade. "You'll no' cut me again, Mistress."

"Only now you see that I could, any time I wish. This is because *I* protect *me*. I do not require your assistance." Mariena released the hilt and lifted her hand to pat his lean cheek. "Go back to the castle, Broden. You should not play at this. You'll only get hurt."

"Play at what, Mistress?" He caught her arm as she moved past him. "Make plain your meaning."

"I think you wish too much to be like the

other men. They are strong, and have the skills to fight, while you…" She paused, realizing how unkind her opinion of him sounded spoken aloud. "You have many other fine qualities, I am sure. Look at your hair. It is perfect."

His fingers tightened. "You think me *weak*?"

Mariena sighed. Now she had put her foot in it.

"Rosealise, she says you catch most of the fish and game for the clan. Your people need food, so this is a very good thing you do." Why was he tugging her back toward the water? "Come now, we will walk back together. It is time to, ah, break the fast with the others, no? And I am hungry now."

"I shall first show you my finest quality." He stopped by the large, flat-topped rock where she had left the housekeeper's soap, which he took and put into her hand. "Stand back and watch."

Taking a few steps away from him, she watched him bend over the huge stone and wrap his arms around it. As it was larger than a cow, and ten times heavier, she couldn't think of what he meant to do.

As he gripped the moss-covered sides with his

hands she grew alarmed. "You do not have to prove–"

Broden picked up the rock as if it weighed no more than a pebble, lifted it high over his head, and tossed it across the river. As it landed with a heavy thud, the ground under Mariena's feet shook.

"Merde alors." She stared at it as it rocked and then settled into the bank, and then turned to see him shaking the moss from his fingers. She'd swear it was a trick of some sort, but earlier she had leaned against the stone, and it hadn't moved a fraction of an inch. "How could you do that?"

"I've the strength of a hundred warriors. I've been thus since we escaped the demons." His gaze shifted over her face. "The chieftain told you how they changed us."

Without their memories, it would be natural for them to assume that. She would have to choose her words carefully now.

"He did not say what sort of abilities they gave you." Mariena walked to the edge of the river to look at the stone, and something occurred to her. "The night I came here, you did not fight me. This is why?"

When Broden didn't answer her, she turned

around to find herself alone again. She shadowed her eyes with her hand before she looked back at the castle, and saw a flicker of movement in the very top of the tower the clan was rebuilding.

It seemed the trapper was not the only one watching her.

Chapter Six

THE CLOUDLESS BLUE summer skies persisting over the highlands kept Galan as earthbound as the Sluath in the days after their battle with the Mag Raith. Without a storm, their wings were useless. Instead they rode on horseback to capture more mortals on their night raids, but Galan took no pleasure in what had become a regular, onerous task. It was almost as loathsome as his current duty. After a long night of listening to the increasingly shrill shrieks coming from the cottage occupied by Prince Iolar, it was time to clean up.

Galan hefted the dead wench's body under his arm, and carried her from the threshold of Iolar's door to the burial pit just outside the village. There he broke the spell covering the mound of bodies heaped inside it, and tossed the fresh corpse atop them. Flies rose in a black cloud from the bodies, buzzing angrily around his head.

Galan frowned at the wench's milky-white eyes staring at him, her mouth still agape in frozen horror. He had removed the cataracts from her eyes, and yet they had reappeared.

"The prince did not care for her joy over having her sight restored," Danar said as he joined him. "But blinding her again brought him great delight. I told him that was that your purpose in healing her, Druid."

"My thanks." He didn't trust a word that came from the big demon's lips, but it cost him nothing to offer words of gratitude. "A pity she didnae last longer."

Galan sealed off the pit again, but as he walked away he took in the scant amount of mortals still alive after the night's revelries. At the rate Prince Iolar was killing the humans they brought for his pleasure, they'd soon empty the local crofts and villages. To find more they'd have to raid more populated territories in the midlands. That would also bring them within the reach of many druid settlements. While Galan doubted his kind could do anything to thwart the Sluath, he had no desire to be captured and delivered to the druid council for disincarnating.

He'd end himself to deny them that victory.

No, what he needed was to learn more details about the Mag Raith, and how they had managed to enter the underworld. That meant consulting with one who had lived during the time of their mortal existence, and had knowledge of the disappearances of the hunters and their tribe. Galan knew by name who had written the original account of both incidents, as he had read it on the scrolls he himself had studied.

Druman of the Emerald Glen tribe would know all that he needed.

Gaining permission to go and consult with a druid required an inventive excuse, but Galan had grown expert at twisting the truth to serve his own needs. He'd also proven his loyalty time and again to the Sluath's prince, who had grown to rely on him as both procurer and advisor in the mortal realm.

"This tree-worshipper would remember a wild tale from a life lived twelve centuries past?" Iolar demanded.

"Druid kind recall every moment of our former incarnations, my prince," Galan reminded him politely. "Druman also wrote the official chronicle of the Mag Raith tribe when they vanished. The conclave demands such records be precise. Much could be gleaned from his memories of that time."

Danar draped Iolar in a fresh white fur before shoving a bundle of blood-soaked garments at a hovering guard. "How will that help us locate the hunters and their women?"

Galan felt a surge of impatience now. "Before writing the scrolls the archivist spoke to other Pritani mortals about the hunters and their people. Those savages died out after the Romans came, so only his memory preserves their accounts." He spread his hands. "Doubtless he'll recall many details that werenae included in the archive scrolls, such as where the hunters went the day they vanished."

"Your kind want you dead," Iolar reminded him. "Not that this would trouble me, but I have invested a good deal of my power in you. Besides that, why would this scribbler tell you anything? You said he doesn't know you."

"I shall show you." With a murmured spell Galan recast his body ward, which shifted and shrank over him like a second skin.

The big demon grunted. "Now I am sincerely not impressed."

"Nor am I." The prince scowled. "You only look older, shorter and fatter."

"In truth, my prince, I look like the head of the druid council," Galan corrected him as he glanced down at his illusion of plain robes over a protruding belly. "I wear the image of Bhaltair Flen, the most powerful conclavist in all of Scotland, as well as the highest authority among druid kind. He's respected and even feared by those of small mind."

"Ah. I remember now." Iolar yawned. "He's also the one who wants you dead. Clever."

Galan sketched a bow of gratitude. "Since this illusion spell draws on your power, my prince, 'tis beyond the ability of druids to detect. Thus, when I order Druman to accompany me, he'll believe me to be Flen, and trot after me with great eagerness. Once I lure him away from his settlement, 'twill be simple to question him until he confides all."

The prince made a languid gesture. "Go then, and do not bring what's left of him back here. Of all mortals, dead druids create the worst stench. That is one reason why I have not killed you."

Chapter Seven

AFTER RETURNING TO the castle to change out of her damp shift, Mariena regarded the new bolt bar on her chamber door. Yesterday when Mael had installed it he'd assured her that the thick wooden crosspiece would keep her room secure while she slept.

"Use your bed for your slumber, my lady," the seneschal said, tucking his hammer into his belt.

Mariena hadn't enjoyed sleeping on the hard, cold stone floor, but personal comfort did not matter to her as much as her safety. The fact that the clan knew about her nightly barricading meant that someone, probably Broden, had come into her room. That he had obviously been appointed as her minder made her situation clear.

She didn't blame Domnall for having her guarded and followed. In his position she would have done the same. She just wished he'd given the task to one of the other men.

Once she changed into the loose tunic and trousers that Jenna had given her, Mariena left her chamber and went to the kitchens. There she found Rosealise finishing the preparations for the morning meal.

"You look very rosy-cheeked today," the housekeeper said as she added some wood to the fire. She stirred a bubbling pot before she regarded Mariena. "The porridge will want another few minutes to cook. Sit down and have a cup with me. I couldn't decide between lemon balm or rosemary to spice up the cornflower, so I've put them all in the blend for the brew."

Suspecting she was about to be lectured on her visit to the river, Mariena took two mugs from the cupboard and brought them to the little table across from the hearth. Yet when Rosealise brought the kettle and filled them, she instead spoke of the work she had to do in the garden.

"From the size of the tops the carrots, they look ready to be pulled, and so do the leeks." She added a small dollop of honey to her brew before offering the pot to Mariena. "I must also grind more oats and barley if I'm to make a blackberry crumble tonight." She frowned at the stone quern sitting on her work table. "What I should give for a proper millhouse. I don't suppose you remember grinding grain, do you?"

"I could try this," Mariena said after sampling the flowery tisane. "But you have plenty of wood and stone here, and the river. With Broden's power, and the water that comes into the castle from the river, you could build your own."

"What a smashing notion. I will speak to Mael and the chieftain about the possibility." Rosealise looked up as Edane and Nellie came in from the hall. "Good morning. My dear, do come and try some of this while I consult with your husband."

Mariena guessed from her prattling about her work that she made the Englishwoman nervous. Jenna also seemed to regard her with the same wariness whenever they spoke, and now so did the archer.

Only Nellie seemed completely at ease as she sat down beside her. "Looks like you found your way to the river for a bath. How can you stand that freezing cold water? It turns my toes blue."

"I wash quickly," Mariena told her, watching

as Edane and Rosealise walked outside. From the hushed tones of their voices they did not wish her to overhear. "Broden followed me there this morning. He was upset and assumed I meant to leave. Why would he think this?"

"That would be because of me." Nellie wrinkled her nose. "I tried to run away—twice."

As the American explained why, she inadvertently answered more of Mariena's unasked questions. Rediscovering the love Nellie and Edane had shared in the underworld had also uncovered the startling truth of the American's secretive past. During their enslavement the other two couples must have formed romantic attachments as well. Their deep affection for each other had been only too plain. Since she had been the last to escape, that meant one of the two men left unattached had likely been her lover.

Kiaran or Broden?

Since the falconer had barely glanced at her, and her Sluath tattoo matched the marks that had been inked on Broden's arm, the answer seemed obvious. Mariena also suspected it as the source of the irresistible pull she felt to the stunning man. He must feel the same attraction, even if he didn't yet realize it or remember her. For a moment she imagined what it would be like, to surrender to such passion and let it fill all the hollowness inside her. Broden, too, would no longer be alone. Her yearning faded as another emotion rose in her: fear, though not for herself.

Whatever they had been to each other in the underworld, Broden needed a woman who could love him. Not one who would have cut his throat in order to make her escape.

Resentment rose like a scalding tide inside Mariena. The traitor should never have put her in this position. By keeping silent about so many things she was actively deceiving the clan. She couldn't find the target, and she couldn't reveal her healing power. She still had not remembered any details of her mission.

For the first time a terrible thought occurred to her. What if the demon sent her here not to kill the watcher, but to help him? Was this clan her target?

"Using bed slaves to help turn mortals into demons is one of the Sluath's favorite tricks," Nellie was saying. "That's why Danar gave Edane to me. He just didn't know that my wickedness—golly, my whole personality—was an act."

What Mariena felt was certainly not a

pretense. Since she had come here she had been on her guard, watching the clan and scouting their castle and its lands. She could not sleep more than a few hours each night, and without weapons at hand she felt naked. Violence did not frighten her. When she thought of the demons, without a qualm she imagined the many ways she could kill them. Even today at the river she had threatened Broden, who had only been watching over her.

The darkness inside her head seemed nothing compared to the blackness that filled her heart. Perhaps that was why the demon had chosen to send her here, because she was as evil as this watcher. That would explain why she'd been told to say nothing to the clan.

"Hey," Nellie said. When Mariena met her gaze, she reached over and touched her hand lightly. "You're going to be okay, Sister. I promise."

"I am well." That was a lie. The sweat inching down her back felt like ice. Still, she knew what she had to do. "It is only that I think I must go. Can you persuade the chieftain to give me a horse and some iron weapons?"

Nellie's smile faded. "The moment you ride

beyond the spell boundary the Sluath will sense you. They'll come for you."

"This is why I need the weapons." She felt the weight of other gazes and looked up to see that Edane and Rosealise had come in, and both frowned at her. "I will hunt the demons," she told them, "and kill as many as I can." She'd slip a knife between her ribs to assure they didn't take her again, either.

"But surely you ken that you belong here with us, Mistress." The archer sat down across from her, his vivid blue eyes filled with concern. "We escaped the underworld together, and now we must fight to remain free. 'Twas plain the night you came to us that you're skilled in fighting. You've much to offer the clan."

"Indeed," the housekeeper chimed in. "And here you will be safe. We know from Nellie that you will likely be attacked the moment you go beyond the boundary. There are too many of them for you to fight by yourself, my dear."

Mariena hadn't expected they would want her to stay. "But I am useless to you, unless you wish more ruined gowns and scorched soup?"

"You're willing to work, my dear," Rosealise said firmly. "That is all anyone may ask of you.

Besides that, there are many tasks here you've not tried. You might be a very accomplished gardener, or skilled at preserving foods. Or perhaps you've done some sort of building work that Jenna may find useful to her efforts."

"You like your garden, your foods and your castle, don't you?" Mariena tried to joke.

"I was a copper in New York City," Nellie said, "working to find the men who killed my brother. You might have done something like that in your time."

"Or I was a murderer." She saw the house-keeper flinch, and the archer recoil, but the little American didn't show any surprise. "You assume I have a good heart, but this is ridiculous. The night I came here, I hurt Broden, and threatened all of you. I was not joking."

"Edane," Nellie said, "would you and Rosealise give us a moment alone, please?"

The archer looked from Mariena to his wife, and something wordless passed between them. He then nodded and walked out of the kitchens with the housekeeper.

"All right, what's eating you, Sister?" the American asked, her directness less friendly now. "You remember something dicey from your past?"

"Before the underworld, no," Mariena admitted. "But Domnall said the demons seek out the wicked and damned to make more of their kind. I may not remember who I was, but I can assure you that I am not innocent or helpless."

"Neither am I." A strange coolness came into Nellie's eyes. "In my time I had to be a very bad gal to get what I wanted—and I was willing to do worse. That's why the Sluath took me."

Mariena glanced at the door. "Did they wish to change you?"

"Yeah, and they wasted over a hundred years trying. I came close, but in the end I would never have let it happen." Her lips curved into a chilling smile. "You understand that."

"I do." In that moment she saw the real woman behind the cheerful façade, and it comforted more than unsettled her. "Your past, this is why you ran?"

"That and Edane," Nellie said. "I thought he deserved better." She blew some air through her lips. "Jeepers, he still deserves it. But I'm going to be that woman, see? I love him, and this clan is my family." Her eyes cooled again. "You should know that I'd do anything to keep them safe. Anything."

Even though she'd made a very unsubtle threat, Mariena felt instantly more at ease. Nellie had taken three arrows in her back to protect her lover, the sort of sacrifice that made her infinitely worthy of Edane.

"These demons," she said to the American, "they are idiots."

"You're not." Nellie leaned closer, her gaze intent. "Listen, doll, be smarter than I was. Whatever you were before, that's done. You can't change it, or go back to your time. What you can do is make a new life here. Work with me today, and we'll see if you ever spent time on a farm. That doesn't suit you, then you can try your luck at building with Jenna. What do you say?"

Her blunt entreaty tempted Mariena. She could certainly control herself. She didn't know what the traitor had sent her to do, but when she finally remembered she did not have to do it. Revealing everything she'd kept secret would not be wise. The chieftain's trust in her would vanish, never to return, but she could find a way to help the clan discover what they didn't yet know. Perhaps with their help she could find her own redemption, as Nellie had.

"Very well. I will stay." Knowing she had an

ally in the American copper made her feel a little less alone. "The others, are any of them like you and me?"

"Kiaran, maybe, but he's been behaving himself. I took him down a couple notches by saving his life during the battle. Long story." She smiled, sliding effortlessly back into her happy carefree persona. "And Broden's not just a pretty face, but you already found that out down at the river."

"You watched from the tower this morning." As the other woman lifted her curled fingers and peered through them Mariena chuckled. "Very clever. So, where did Broden go, and why did he leave so quickly?"

Nellie winked. "You'll have to ask him about that."

Chapter Eight

AFTER SNARING AND hooking enough game to keep the clan well-fed for weeks, Broden returned to the stronghold. On his way he spied Mariena out in the cow pasture with Nellie and Jenna. Since the three women appeared to be inspecting the herd, which would take some time, he went to the smokehouse, where he cleaned, wrapped and hung the meat and fish over a green wood fire.

Working gave him a chance to think on something other than the Frenchwoman. He never wasted any part of the animals that sustained them. The furs of the rabbits he would scrape and stretch so they could be made into boot linings and blankets for winter. Even the fish heads and innards he would chop and bury in Rosealise's gardens to nourish her plants.

Yet even as he processed the fine catch, he felt his aversion growing. Like the other Mag Raith, he had come to despise hunting, and made it his practice to take only what they needed. Washing the blood from his hands, Broden came to an uneasy realization. With all the meat he'd taken he'd have nothing to do until the next moon.

"Now I've facked myself," he muttered.

"That I shouldnae enjoy seeing," Edane said. He came in, stopped, and cast a measuring look overhead. "By the Gods. 'Tis anything left in the forest or river?"

"Why dinnae you go and see?" Broden eyed some trout that had finished curing, and took down two large fillets. When he glanced at the archer he saw worry in his gaze, and stiffened. "What now? Mariena–"

Edane held up his hand. "She's well, Brother. I but wished to tell you that my lady and Jenna shall look after her for the remainder of the day." He nodded at the trout. "'Tis for Kiaran?"

"His fondness for cured fish rivals that of the Norsemen." Broden wrapped the fillets in some birch bark. "Hasnae he fully recovered from the battle?"

"His wounds, aye." Edane looked as if he wished to say more, and then simply nodded to him and left.

Broden added some boughs to the smoking fire, assuring it wouldn't go out. The scent of the smoldering spruce followed him to the half-ruined tower Kiaran had retreated to after the battle with the demons.

Two kestrels perched on newly-mortared stones in the half-fallen, circular wall. They puffed up their chest feathers and stretched their necks, both glaring at him with their customary disdain. Knowing the birds would attack him if they thought him a threat to Kiaran, Broden held up the wrapped fish.

"I bring food, not trouble."

The female raptor made a sharp sound, and then turned her head as Kiaran appeared behind her, his body wrapped in a thick blanket.

"Quiet, Dive." The falconer looked little better than he had just after the battle, and his eyes stared with a flatness that seemed chillier than his usual remoteness. "I dinnae need coddling, Brother."

"I'd give you a clout to the head, but 'twould make more work for Edane. The fish, 'tis tastier." Broden stepped through the gap in the stones and walked past the other man. "What do you out here, besides sulk?"

"Sleep. Think." Kiaran pulled aside a large blanket hung from the remains of an arch. "See for yourself."

Within the tower the falconer had made a bed chamber of sorts, primarily occupied with a rope pallet of lashed boughs covered with fleeces. A pail of water sat beside the rough bed, as did his sheathed sword and some hand tools. A faded tartan stretched over the space like a tent roof, from which he'd hung some bunches of dried herbs. The falconer had even fashioned a fire-place by stacking flat stones in one of the gaps in the tower's outer wall to form the hearth, and channeled the smoke out through a mud and stone flue. The remainder of his kestrels sat on perches fashioned from thin branches inserted into the wall seams.

"A pleasant hideout," Broden said. It also looked very familiar. "If you've concealed dried berries, filched meat, and dead voles under that pallet, then I reckon you're reliving your boyhood. What next? Raids on Rosealise's veg crops?"

"I've no need to steal food. 'Tis brought to me daily." Kiaran took the trout from him. "This day pottage from Lady Rosealise, a basket of wild strawberries from Lady Jenna, and all the ptarmigan who crossed Dive's path." He nodded toward a spit of three birds over the hearth fire. "Mayhap I shall deliver the excess to Mael for the clan. Gods ken I've naught else to offer but more trouble."

"Excess I've seen to, Brother," Broden said but heard the deep sadness behind Kiaran's jest. "Summer's bounty shallnae last forever. Nor shall Domnall's ire on your mistrust of Lady Nellie. Return to the stronghold. If for naught but the granary has a better roof, and walls to keep out the wind." He hesitated. "You're missed by more than me."

"'Tis growing crowded, and I'm happier here." Kiaran's mouth hitched as he filled two cups with brew, and handed one to Broden. "How fares your Francian lady?"

"She's no' mine," Broden corrected, "and her people call themselves French in their time." The abrupt change of subject seemed worrying, too, but he went along with it. “She’s well. Domnall has kept naught from her, and the other females make her welcome. She remembers some of her time in the underworld.”

“But no’ you.” The falconer leaned back against the wall, and lifted his mug. “Mayhap ’twill soon change. You were right about her, for you bear the same ink.”

Broden should have said aye, and left it at that, but Kiaran remained his closest friend among the clan.

“Until this morning the lady thought me but a pretty lad. She bid me take satisfaction in that I’m a fine trapper, and a pleasure to behold.” He told him about the encounter at the river, and then met the other man’s gaze. “I’ve no’ otherwise impressed her. She even advised me I’m too weak to serve as a proper warrior.”

The falconer choked on his brew, and had to clear his throat. “Gods. You dispelled that notion by hurling the rock, I’ll wager?”

“Aye.” Recalling her shock when he’d thrown the boulder should have made him feel prideful, but it had done nothing about his quandary. “’Tis clear she doesnae regard me favorably. I’m glad I’ve yet to speak to her of the dreams.”

"I cannae fathom why you'd dare. She might take a blade to you again—and aim lower." Kiaran stroked his chin as Broden glared at him. "You ken, I've no' yet ruined my chances with the lady, and Dun Chaill provides little amusement. Mayhap I should alter my skinwork, or try dreaming of her."

"Aye, as you've ever done so well with females." Broden started to leave, stopped and turned back to him. "Edane claims you're well, but he seemed strange when he said thus to me. Does he lie, then?"

"My battle wounds healed that night," the falconer said, averting his gaze.

His friend's secretive ways usually didn't annoy Broden, but his moving to the tower seemed more than a wish for solitude. He could also see sweat dotting Kiaran's upper lip, as if he felt nervous. "Facking tell me in truth what's wrong, you stubborn arse, or by the Gods I shall beat it out of you." The falconer looked at him for a long moment. "You've done the same for me," Broden reminded him, "including the beating."

"Galan's attack didnae wound me. 'Tis that which unsettles the shaman, and keeps me to the tower." Kiaran ducked his head. "I've changed, Broden."

"How so?" He peered at him. "You look the same to me."

The falconer reached for the bottom of his tunic, pulling it over his head before he turned around to show his back.

Broden took in a quick breath as he saw the down-covered protrusions sprouting from Kiaran's shoulder blades. Made of flesh, each stretched as long as a man's forearm, and arched up before curving down. "'Tisnae possible."

"Yet 'tis as you see." The falconer looked at his kestrels. "I now grow wings."

Chapter Nine

THE DUST OF the road wafted around Galan as he reined in his mount and regarded the emptiness of the glen before him. Mortals perceptive enough to notice the faint shimmer in the air would think it nothing more than summer heat. But the road veered off too abruptly, as if to avoid the thick grasses of the open meadows. Galan dismounted, taking care to fumble a bit as he did, and affected a limp as he approached the two scraggly oaks standing like sentinels at the glen's border.

The Emerald Glen tribe's settlement lay just beyond them.

Behind him he felt the tingle of a Sluath presence, and wondered who followed him, and why. If Prince Iolar had sent someone to follow him, it would be Danar, the only one among his demons that he truly trusted. If another had decided to track him for other reasons, then it might be any of the prince's lieutenants.

Dealing with his demonic shadow would have to wait.

Bhaltair Flen would stop politely outside any settlement and wait to be greeted, as the old fool greatly concerned himself with such archaic manners. To maintain his ruse, Galan did the same, and amused himself by imagining what he would do to Flen once he had found Culvar, and obtained the secret of eternal life. He wanted the smug bastart to suffer greatly before he ended him, and he had learned the methods of inflicting terror on mortal kind. They would not have the same effect on an old, wily soul like Flen, but perhaps Culvar could aid him in that as well.

The shimmer in the air grew to a glitter, and then a young shepherdess stepped out from behind one of the oaks. A handful of young lambs followed her as she walked toward him, their small tails wagging.

"Fair day, Marster," she said, dropping into a crofter's bob. "Ye've left the road to the midlands. What seek ye here?"

Galan held back a sigh as he bowed to her. "I am Bhaltair Flen, head of the conclave. I've come to speak with the archivist Druman on a matter of great urgency, Sister." There, that sounded pompous enough, even to his own ears.

"Indeed." Her smile faded along with the illusion cloaking her, revealing her to be a much older woman with silver-streaked brown hair. The lambs disappeared as she planted her crook, which now shifted into a golden scythe. "We had no word by dove of your visit, Master Flen."

Her voice trembled slightly as she spoke, betraying either fear or weariness.

"'Twas no time for messaging. Forgive my haste, but it couldnae be helped." He considered killing her, but that would summon the rest of the tribe's defenders, and he would have to waste more of his power and time ending them. He tucked his hands into the sleeves of his robes and took on a tone of long-suffering patience. "Shall I wait while you advise your headman of my arrival, and obtain permission for my entry?"

"I should never deny you, Master Flen. Forgive me." She bowed deeply. "Come this way."

The space between the two oaks darkened for a moment as the druidess removed the protective spell, and a small settlement appeared in the center of the glen. Surrounding it were groves of trees draped heavily with enchanted mistletoe, forming a protective boundary. Pens of livestock and broad gardens of herbs and vegetables surrounded the glen. Dozens of druids working with the animals and the crops looked up as the druidess led Galan into the settlement. The younger of them did not conceal their worry.

"'Tis been some trouble here, Sister?" he asked.

"We trade with some villages to the east of the midlands. Over the last weeks our brothers found each one emptied of mortals. They left their crops to rot, and their stock to starve." She glanced at him. "We sent word to the council, you ken, but havenae received an answer."

He nodded, pleased to have been given the excuse. "Then you ken my mission, Sister. 'Tis why I've come."

A middle-aged man emerged from a barn and strode toward them, his robes pelted with straw and bits of wool. From the aura of power he shed, Galan knew he was the tribe's headman. Yet he, too, appeared overly-wary.

"Welcome, Brother," the headman said,

looking from him to the druidess, who gave him a small nod. "How may we serve?"

Even better for Galan, the headman didn't recognize his illusion, which meant he did not know Bhaltair Flen personally. After introducing himself, he asked, "I've come to speak with your archivist, Druman, about a matter he chronicled in the days of the Roman invaders. 'Tis vital that I glean every detail he recalls."

"Druman." The headman cleared his throat. "Well, then I shall take you to my cottage, that you may speak there. Go and fetch the lad for Master Flen, Sister. Come, Master."

Galan followed the other druid to a modest cottage, in which he was presented to the druid's mate and eldest son. He had never realized how tiresome the rituals of greeting and welcome were until now, and wondered how he had ever tolerated them as headman of the Moss Dapple. Doubtless Aklen had taken his place since he'd been banished. Once he attained immortality he would have to return to the enchanted forest and deal with the arrogant, meddling shaman. Indeed, he would take pleasure in taking vengeance against every member of his former tribe for turning against him.

The druidess returned, accompanied by a child no more than three or four years old. Impatient now, Galan glanced past her but saw no one else entering. "You didnae find him?"

"She did, sir," the headman said uneasily.

"My name is Druman," the boy said, piping the words in his baby's voice. "What do you want to ken?"

Chapter Ten

MARIENA SPENT THE rest of the morning learning about the clan's herds and flocks from Nellie, who had a deft touch with the animals and seemed to know everything about caring for them. Very quickly Mariena discovered she did not share her talents. For the remainder of the day she worked alongside Jenna as they cleared debris from one of the passages. The architect explained in more detail the work in progress on the castle as they carried baskets of deadfall, rotted leaves and other detritus out to a large fire pit.

"How did you make out with the livestock?" Jenna asked as they emptied the last baskets into the flames.

"I can make the cows all run away from me,

very fast," Mariena admitted, scissoring her fingers through the air to demonstrate the speed of the skittish herd. "The chickens and quail try to fly from me. But the sheep hate me. When I come close they make ugly sounds, and crowd together, and charge at me."

"They do that to everyone. Mael says they get cranky after lambing season." She looked past her and sighed. "Look at that."

The setting sun filtered through the trees, the bright circle sinking into a band of gold, orange and purple between the earth and sky. More light formed streamers that slanted through the branches and leaves, gilding the forest with unearthly beauty. Through those beams birds darted and thistledown floated, catching bits of the glow on their wings and fluff.

It felt to Mariena as if they stood somewhere out of time, in some secret world held together by eternal, exquisite magic. "I begin to appreciate your attachment to this place."

"It's a strange thing," Jenna said, her tone as dreamy as her eyes. "Before the Sluath grabbed me all I ever cared about was my work. I wanted to become a world-renown architect and design important, brilliant buildings all over the globe.

My ambition cost me everything. I nearly died for it, too. Seems almost silly now."

"Yet here you are," Mariena said, amused, "the architect of Dun Chaill."

"Oh, don't get me wrong. I love doing this restoration. To rebuild an actual working medieval castle is an incredible experience. But I think I'd be just as happy building half a dozen cottages for the clan." The architect smiled at her as she turned back toward the stronghold. "Naturally they'd be important, brilliant cottages."

"But of course."

Mariena fell into step beside her, but as she tucked her empty basket under her arm the scent of the fire pit took on a different note, like that of bread. A vision of another, smaller basket filled with baguettes flashed through her thoughts, but it had been attached to something…metal bars… the front of a bicycle…

The pain that instantly swept away the memory felt like a punch to her temple, but Mariena expected it this time, and endured it to see if her power would lessen the discomfort. As soon as the details began to fade she tried to recall the bicycle and the basket of bread again, and more images came to her.

"Mariena, are you all right?" she heard Jenna say, as if she stood at the opposite end of a long tunnel.

The images blurred, and she shook her head as she closed her eyes. "Give me a moment, *ma copine*."

The vision returned, and all around her she saw the narrow streets of Paris. On the bicycle she held she saw a blue, red and silver emblem with a growling cat and the word FAVOR. Behind it weeds poked through the rusting rungs of an old iron fence. Beyond that stood a timeworn villa sandwiched between two taller buildings. The curtained panes of the building's windows glittered with new frost.

Looking at the building made Mariena taste bile in her mouth. It should have seemed lovely, but regarding it made her want to be sick. Something terrible lay curled inside its walls, like some horrendous, ravenous beast waiting to devour anyone who dared come inside. Yet she was walking toward it now.

Her gaze drifted up. Between two windows at the top of the building hung something red and black that blurred as tears filled her eyes. The black began to spread like rot, seeping into the graying fascia, which began to crumble. A hooded face came into her sight, two glowing white eyes appearing in the shroud's darkness.

Your fight is not here, mortal.

Pain shattered the world, plunging Mariena into a darkness so absolute she thought she must be dead. Then she felt gentle hands on her face, and heard an urgent voice, calling her from the void. Opening her eyes felt as startling as taking in a breath. The tops of trees clustered above her, and it took another moment to realize she lay on her back in the grass.

"Mariena, can you hear– Oh, good." Jenna, who kneeled over her, made a sound of relief. "Are you all right? You passed out."

"Bon sang." Mariena grimaced as she sat up, and pressed a cold hand to her aching skull. "A memory came back to me, and then the pain. I held onto it, and I saw a little more. Does this happen to you?"

"Generally I don't hold onto memories until I faint. Okay, easy, now." The other woman helped her to her feet and put a steadying arm around her waist. "Let's get you back inside."

Domnall met them before they reached the stronghold, at which point Mariena stepped away from Jenna to test her legs. Jenna quickly told her husband about the faint.

"I shall summon Edane," the chieftain said, and reached as if to lift her into his arms.

Mariena thought if he touched her she might start sobbing, and quickly stepped out of his reach. "Thank you, Monsieur, but I can walk. My head aches only a little. It was much worse after I fell from the sky. I will go and rest in my room. Do not trouble your shaman."

Jenna insisted on accompanying her, and once inside her chamber still appeared worried. "Please, let me go and get Edane. He's got some awesome headache potions, and you look really pale."

"With this skin, that is always my look." She sat down on the edge of the small bed.

The architect hovered as she watched her. "Did you remember the demons taking you? Those are usually the worst ones."

"No, I remembered being in Paris. I had a fine, new bicycle with a basket filled with many loaves of bread. I think I was making a delivery." She decided against describing the other, more disturbing images she'd seen, or the fear she'd felt. "What does that tell you?"

"Only that you're probably from the twentieth century," Jenna said slowly. "With time I'm sure you'll remember more. All of us have. It's just that we don't know anything about the spell the Sluath used on us to steal our memories, or the consequences of fighting it. Edane thinks it could be very dangerous."

"You mean the next time I try that I might not wake up." As the American nodded Mariena rubbed her forehead. "I despise this."

"I know how that helplessness feels, too. Anyway, it's about time for the evening meal. Are you hungry?" When she shook her head, Jenna went to the door. "I'll have Rosealise keep something warm, in case you want to eat later. In the meantime, try to get some rest."

As soon as the chieftain's wife left, Mariena dropped back on the bed and pulled the feather pillow over her face. She wanted to scream into it. She wanted to tear it to pieces. The clan thought that the Sluath had taken their memories. She should tell them it had been the work of the traitor. Yet each time she came close to doing so, something inside her gripped her heart in tight, merciless claws.

You must tell no one.

No spell kept her silent, of that Mariena was convinced. She could go out in the great hall, and sit down with the clan, and end their ignorance. She could explain that the Sluath had not changed the Mag Raith, nor had Dun Chaill resurrected their women. She could tell them that she had healed Nellie, and Broden, and everything more she remembered. Yet even as she convinced herself to rise from the bed and do those very things, she realized why she couldn't.

It is not yet the time for them to know.

She found herself wishing Broden was beside her on the bed. Aside from the welcome distraction he would provide—how could a woman tire of looking at him—his presence would comfort her. She always felt something ease inside her whenever he came near.

What would he think of her keeping secrets from the clan?

Her hands pushed aside the pillow, and Mariena stared up at the beams overhead. There was nothing she could do but wait. Closing her eyes brought relief, and then a deepening darkness, and a welcome oblivion.

Chapter Eleven

AT THE EVENING meal Broden kept eyeing the empty place across the table where Mariena usually sat, but said nothing. Instead he listened as the others talked of the day's work. Asking about the lady would only remind the clan of his obsession with her. He had to wait and hope someone would mention why the Frenchwoman had not joined them.

Why would she stay away? Had his show of strength at the river frightened her? He should never have done that. She might think he couldn't control himself. Was that the reason?

As he picked at his food and brooded his clan's discussions began to needle him as well. Nellie praised Edane's milking skills, and reported one of the hens had hidden away and hatched a clutch of chicks in the barn loft. The women discussed this as if she had found a hoard of gold. Mael next spoke of his progress in preparing more space in the vegetable garden for planting, for which Rosealise said she had started cabbage, squash and wild garlic plants ready to leave the greenhouse. Domnall asked after Kiaran, who also continued to avoid the hall, but Edane said he was still recovering.

By the time Jenna spoke of the passage she and Mariena had cleared Broden thought he might grind his back teeth down to the roots.

"We cleared and burned the last of the debris, so we should start on the roof supports tomorrow," the chieftain's wife said. "I'll rig some chain hoists, but we'll need some safety lines, too."

"'Tis better to drive the nails partway into the beams on the ground before we raise them," Mael put in. "'Twill take less time to hammer them once they're in place. Did Kiaran forge enough?"

"What of Kiaran's back?" Broden finally demanded. As the archer eyed him he made an impatient gesture. "He showed me the growths, Edane. The rest of the clan should ken."

"All of us do, my dear sir," Rosealise said gently.

They knew, but they had not told him, and Broden could not fathom why. "Yet you said naught to me."

"'Twas his decision," Domnall said, looking blandly at him. "Kiaran reckoned you've enough to worry on, and I agreed."

His best friend and the chieftain thought him weak. Broden felt his temper begin to simmer even higher. "'Tis anything more you secret from me?"

"After her faint I don't think Mariena should do any work tomorrow," Jenna said carefully. "Especially heavy lifting, so if–"

"She swooned?" Broden hadn't meant to snarl the words, or jerk out of his seat, so he added, "Forgive me, my lady, but what caused that?"

"Mistress Douet tried to force a remembrance," Domnall answered for his wife. "She roused from the swoon after a few moments. It but left her with an aching head. She didnae wish me to fetch Edane, and took to her bed to rest."

"She was a little pale, but otherwise she seemed fine," Jenna put in as Broden came around the table. "I was planning to check on her again, but maybe you could do that," she called after him.

He felt the others staring at him as he stalked out, and found he didn't care. They should never have left her alone, not in such a state. Unlike the rest of them she was still mortal. What if she needed aid, and could not call for help?

By the time Broden reached Mariena's chamber he had envisioned all manner of sickness and calamity befalling her, which swept all but the need to see her from his thoughts. If he had to kick down her door, so he would. Yet when he took hold of the latch it opened freely. He hurried inside the shadowy chamber. She had not dropped the bolt bar to secure herself, as she had done every night, so surely that meant–

The door slammed shut behind him. At the same moment something heavy and wooden rammed into his left knee, knocking him off balance, and then swung up to smash into his chin, sending him careening backward.

Broden ended up on his back with Mariena standing over him. She hefted a length of firewood over her head as she stared down at him and muttered something long and vicious-sounding in her native tongue.

"You're well, then, my lady," he said, rubbing his jaw but making no move to rise.

"I am fine, *imbécile*." She threw the split back on the pile by the hearth before she planted her hands on her hips. "But you should have a broken head. What are you doing, barging in this way?"

Broden couldn't admit to the state he'd worked himself into. "You didnae bar the door."

"I fell asleep," Mariena said. "It is night, no? The time for sleeping."

"Jenna said you fainted." He propped himself up, and became entranced as he met her gaze. In his dreams he'd never seen her eyes glow as they did now, as if they had been dipped in a sunset. *Gods, fool, take hold of yourself.* "'Tis good to ken that you're well."

"But now you are not." She took a flaming twig from the fire and used it to light the oil lamp by her pallet. By then he'd gotten to his feet, and she came over to peer at his face and leg. "*Merde alors*. You are the mess."

Broden tried to surreptitiously wipe what was dripping from his chin. "You didnae hurt me."

"You are bleeding because you feel fine? No," she added as he started for the door, and pointed to her narrow bed. "I injured your leg, and I will fix it. Sit down."

He tried not to limp, but the leg she had

coshed did not want to bend. "Call for Edane, and he'll tend to me."

"Be quiet." She brought the lamp over to inspect his leg before she set it aside and positioned herself an arm's length in front of him. "I knocked your knee out of joint. Give me your foot." When he didn't move she made an impatient sound and reached for his boot. "This will hurt. You will shout."

"My lady, you neednae–"

He yelped as she yanked sharply on his leg, and his knee made a loud popping sound. A ferocious spear of pain jammed up into his thigh, only to fade as she clamped her hand over his knee.

Mariena dropped down beside him, her fists clenched and her shoulders hunched. She took in a deep breath and closed her eyes. "Done. You should leave now."

Broden saw how she was trembling, and touched her arm. "Do you feel faint again?"

"Faint?" Her mouth thinned, and she dropped her chin as her shoulders shook. He thought she was weeping, and then a sound slipped from her that told him otherwise. She was trying not to laugh.

Females had admired him, lusted after him—

some had even feared him—but none had ever laughed at him.

"Désolé." Mariena rubbed her fingers against her eyes, but when she saw his puzzled look, she translated. "I am sorry, Broden. I do not think you are funny. You are kind to me, and I hurt you, twice." She looked at him. "You will forgive me?"

How she got on his lap, Broden couldn't say. Nor had he any explanation for how his hands now framed her face, or the feel of her heart beating against his. Whether she meant what she said or not, she wasn't laughing at him now. The blue of her eyes darkened, while the gold patches flared like torch fire. Her full lips parted a little, and soft rosy color pinked her pale cheeks.

All he could do then was tell her what he'd wanted since the moment he'd seen her fall from the sky. "I shall…if you kiss me."

The pain ebbing from her own knee no longer concerned Mariena. Healing the Scotsman so openly had been stupid of her, but she had inflicted his injury. While his immortal healing ability took care of the wounded jaw, the dislocation was something that had to be righted.

Though she had collapsed onto his lap, in another moment she could push him away. She would be able to stand and move without limping, and tell him to leave. He wouldn't discover her power, and her secret would remain safe, and she could work on discovering why she had been sent here.

Only none of that mattered to her in the slightest.

Broden held her face between his hands, which were as beautiful as the rest of him, but it was his touch that made her forget to breathe. His flesh felt smooth and warm against her skin, yet the way he looked at her ignited a branded heat that raced through her face. As it spread down her throat and into her breasts, she realized he thought her just as captivating as she regarded him. She wanted her lips on him, this stunning man, who could have any woman he desired, and probably had.

Yet Broden didn't want any woman. He wanted her.

He had become infatuated with her, Mariena told herself sternly, because he felt lonely, and she was the only unattached female at Dun Chaill. Still, it tugged at her, his longing, as if it were some secret he'd kept from everyone. What kind of man wanted a woman who might have crippled him, broken his jaw, or cut his throat?

"You are deranged," she told him.

"Mayhap." Broden lifted her off his thighs, setting her on her feet before he stood and put his hands on her waist. "Yet you wish to kiss me, dinnae you?"

What she wanted was to bolt the door, and take off her clothes, and take him to bed. She wanted to give herself to him for the rest of the night. She would allow him to touch and caress and do whatever he liked to her. The violence of that hunger for him shook her, for it felt like something she would happily kill to have. To let down her guard, something she never did, seemed something she could only do with him.

"I'm mistaken, then." His hands tightened for a moment. "I'll go."

Mariena had already curled her hand around his neck, and breathed in the last word he spoke. *Go* tasted like a sip of some luscious golden wine, and letting herself drink it down, she pressed her lips to his. The first shock came from discovering that their mouths matched perfectly, as if designed to do nothing more than kiss each other.

Broden made a rough sound in his throat, and used his lips to nudge hers apart.

Oh, but she should not have done this, Mariena thought, her body exploding with countless nerves coming alive and clamoring for more of him. The feel of his tongue stroking the inner curves of her lips felt so exquisite she moaned against the wet, satiny caress. Had he kissed other women like this? She would hurt him again if he had. The edge of his teeth grazed her bottom lip, setting off another drenching flood of sensation that cascaded down her torso and gathered into a pulsing pool between her thighs.

What are you doing? You have no time for indulging him or yourself.

To allow the kiss to continue when she knew too much, and Broden nothing of her, seemed supremely foolish. He might look as beautiful as the demons, but he had no cruelty in him. He wouldn't toss her on the bed, or drag her to the ground. Like the other men he had been polite and careful. He would ask her permission before he put his hands on her. He wouldn't have stolen so much as this kiss.

Broden proved her wrong as he pulled her closer, his hands spreading over her back.

Mariena felt the heat of his body fully now, and that set her legs to trembling. Her knee no longer hurt, but she couldn't feel the other one now, either. She would be sensible and make him go in another moment, after she stopped herself from clutching his shoulders, after he ended this terrible, blissful thing he was doing to her mouth with his tongue. How was it still kissing? It felt like sex, like the most dangerous, forbidden of intimacies. Enthralling and terrifying and so addictive she knew soon she would be helpless to stop him from doing anything he wished to her.

Why should I stop him? I love this.

One of them made a low, guttural sound, and the other answered with a groan. Broden tightened his hold as he took the kiss from tasting to claiming.

Demanding desire flashed through Mariena, so passionate and volcanic now she thought her bones might dissolve. She could not allow him to take her over, to possess her. But it was still only a kiss. Just their mouths pressed together. Just his tongue thrusting against hers. Just that and nothing more, except that now she couldn't breathe or move away, not now, not ever again.

If he stops I will die.

Her body shivered and shook as if she stood naked in neck-deep snow, unable to escape, slowly freezing to death. But the heat of him fired the same in her. Flames of wanting filled her mind, burning away all rational thought. Something deep in her belly expanded, starving and savage, demanding things she couldn't do with a man she'd known for a handful of days. A man who was not her lover, who could snap her in two if he wished, and she could never, ever stop him from kissing her like this.

Broden wrenched his mouth from hers and glanced at her narrow bed. As he brought her wrist to his face and rubbed it against his cheek, he said, "Come to my chamber, *a thasgaidh.*"

Mariena could barely make out the words for the harsh rasp of his voice, and the deafening roar in her head. "What?"

"*A thasgaidh,*" he repeated, "my darling one." He dipped his head, his silky dark hair caressing her face as he murmured against her ear. "I'd have you. Naked against me, in my bed. Atop me. Under me. You desire me the same. I want to taste you, pleasure you. Come with me, and I shall."

He sounded drunk, Mariena thought, or unbalanced. Since she felt the same way, and nothing else affected them, they were doing this to each other—by *kissing*.

"I cannot. I…" Why did she sound as if she were begging for him? "You do not know me. We cannot do this."

When he didn't reply. she drew back her free hand and slapped him. It was, she thought, much better than slapping herself.

The change in him came so fast it felt as if he'd done the same to her. He jerked her hands from his shoulders and pushed her to arm's length, his chest rising and falling rapidly as he stared at her.

"No," Broden breathed. He caught her wrist when she tried to move away. "Look at me." His other hand went to her jaw and gently turned her head. "'Tis your power, to enthrall a man thus, with but a kiss?"

He thought her responsible? Now she might punch him in that stunning face.

"I did what you asked," she reminded him as she tried to collect herself. "I kissed you. That is all it was. What happened…" She had no words for it.

Broden peered at her, his body tensing and his hands tightening around her wrist and jaw. For a moment Mariena thought he might fling her over his shoulder and carry her off to his bed. Now that she thought about it, becoming his lover seemed worth it. Just kissing him had brought her to the brink of climax. To take him inside her might kill her, but what a death that would be. Consuming, glorious, like burning alive in an inferno of bliss.

She wanted him so badly that despite her fear of what they were doing to each other, and all that she couldn't remember, she was talking herself into it anyway. Worse, this now seemed sensible.

"Do you ken me?" He shoved her hand inside his tunic, against the hard wall of his chest. "From the underworld?"

Mariena had no memory of him at all before falling from the sky. Of that she was certain. "I remember us at the sky bridge. All the clan. But you alone, with me, *mon ange*…" She shook her head.

"Yet still you wish to bed me." Broden closed

his eyes for a moment, and when he looked at her again, a weariness came into his expression. “Dinnae blame yourself. ’Tis the same with all females. They look upon me, and cannot help their desire.”

Is that what he thought, that his magnificence drew her to him?

“You are very handsome, but that means nothing to me. How you make me feel seduces me, not your face or your body. You could be an ogre and I would want you, Broden. ” She touched his mouth. “Kissing you almost enslaved *me*.”

What she said made something hot flare into his eyes.

He pressed her fingers against his lips, and then repeated the caress on her palm. “What shall we do, then, my lady?”

Chapter Twelve

IN THE HEDGEROWS behind Dun Chaill, Cul emerged from his hidden underground entry, and listened for a long moment before he limped out of the maze trap. He knew from his listening post that the clan had retired for the night, leaving their shaman on watch inside the keepe. Only the falconer's kestrels patrolled the exterior of the castle, and they could not see through the shroud of Cul's warding shadows. As long as he moved slowly, and disturbed nothing in his path, he could move about freely.

Freely, but in agony.

He could do little more than drag his shattered leg now, and had been obliged to fashion a crutch for himself to avoid falling even in the tunnels. The pain of the wrongly-healed injury plagued him even when he took to his bed. He dare not stray far from Dun Chaill, nor could he send out his iron warriors when he needed them to guard his underground warren against the Mag Raith. The perpetual grinding his weight placed on the badly-knitted bones, he suspected, would soon render him so crippled he could not bear to walk.

He would have to take Mariena soon, but he had to know the extent of her transference ability.

Outside the half-ruined tower Cul stopped to avoid stepping into a pool of torchlight. His eyes narrowed as he saw the falconer sitting atop the remains of a wall. He stared up at the night sky, his expression revealing nothing of his thoughts. The bulky cape of wool he wore, however, bulged over the back of his shoulders in a telling fashion. Seeing that made Cul feel the nubs that remained of his own, stunted wings rise like hackles.

He clamped down on his outrage. Killing Kiaran before he finished this startling change would provide him with great pleasure, but it might also rouse his clan to seek vengeance. He was in no state to take on the other four immortals. Once he had been healed, he could devise a fitting end for the falconer.

One of the kestrels swooped down to land on Kiaran's shoulder. The little raptor nudged his cheek and chittered at him as if speaking.

"'Tis naught to hunt tonight, Dive." Absently he caressed her head as he looked down and by chance stared directly into Cul's eyes. "'Tis time to end this."

Could the hunter hear his thoughts? For a moment Cul imagined if he could, and a strange sensation gathered in his chest. He'd murdered every mortal who'd ever lain eyes on him, or who might expose his presence at Dun Chaill. All had been necessary, but some still haunted him, like the old man he'd found slowly dying in Wachvale after the druid and his mercenaries had attacked the place. He had apologized to the mortal for stealing the last minutes of his wretched life.

Before that he had not spoken to anyone for more than a thousand years.

Cul let himself recall that last, furtive conversation in the underworld, with the strange female who had set him on his path to escape. He remembered seeing her slip into his cell, and feeling revolted when she made to release his shackles. The most cherished of all the Sluath slaves, everything about her repelled him, especially as he knew exactly who she was. Yet like any male who gazed upon her, he felt the pull of her tugging at him, as a flickering candle did the moth.

Prince Iolar means to end the king tonight, and take the throne, the slave told him. *Ye must flee to the mortal realm now, or he shall murder ye, too. I shall aid ye.*

He'd laughed at her. *Why would you save me, little mortal?*

The slave ignored his question and took out a scroll, on which had been drawn a crude map. *Go here, Culvar, and ye shall find all ye need to live.*

What need I live for? he said, mocking her.

That for which ye've endured each hour of yer miserable life here. Her smile did not reach her eyes. *Vengeance.* When he reached for the scroll his manacles rattled, and she moved it out of his reach. *In return for my aid, ye shall make a vow to me.*

What she had asked of him had been so ridiculous that Cul had laughed at her again. Why make a promise of something he'd already sworn to himself never to do again? Yet in the end he had given her his word, convinced he would never have to break it.

The kestrel flew up into the trees as Kiaran suddenly leapt down from the wall, landing only a short distance from Cul. Instead of attacking him, however, he turned away and retreated into the ruined tower.

Feeling sullen now, Cul retreated into the forest, and there followed the trail used by the trapper when checking his snares in the brush. Each one he found empty until he reached a patch of blaeberry shrubs laden with ripe berries, in which Broden had set two rabbit traps. He crouched down, wincing as the movement jarred his leg, and studied the flip snares, to which he had tied two tree branches.

These would serve his purpose admirably.

From his tunic he took the common carrot plant he had stolen from the clan's garden, pushing it into the ground before he poured a vial over it. The spell he then murmured caused the stalks to thicken, and clusters of white flowers to sprout. Covering his hand with a cloth, he carefully wound the plant into the snare. The last touch required his dagger, which he used to cut the trigger cord until only a single thread held it in place.

Satisfied with his work, Cul warded the area

around the traps to prevent any creatures from coming near it.

On his way back to the maze he avoided the ruined tower, unwilling to tempt himself again. He saw through the trees the flicker of light from within the outcast's new home, and heard a sharp sound of pain. Through the air came the acrid stench of flesh and feathers burning. Agony followed in a stream of suffering, and Cul breathed it in like the perfume of rare blossoms. He had missed this most of all, but that wasn't the point.

It seemed Kiaran had changed his mind, and he wouldn't have to kill him.

Chapter Thirteen

BRODEN OPENED THE door to his chamber, and followed Mariena inside. The embers of the fire he'd banked glowed orange-red in the hearth, but only the torch he'd taken from the hall pushed back the darkness. It showed her the work table where he sketched his notions for traps, and the coils of cording he wove for his snares. He kept his few garments and spare boots stowed in a trunk beneath his bench. An upright log held the basin he used for washing by the wide bed he'd built of pine and rope. Aside from his sword and daggers, which he now removed from his belt and set on the table, he had no other possessions. Dwelling with four brothers among a tribe of *dru-wids*, he'd never thought on it. Now it seemed to shout silently of his inadequacy.

He could do nothing to make himself seem worthy of her, for he knew he'd never be.

As he put the torch in the wall bracket above his bed Broden felt as if he'd again stepped into a dream. The torchlight cast gold in her hair and on her skin, warming the paleness of her, making her seem even less real. So many nights he'd imagined her here with him. Would Mariena vanish the moment he touched her, as she had each time he'd awakened?

It had been like a dream when she'd agreed to share his bed. Now it felt like torture.

Mariena turned around slowly, taking everything in before she regarded him. "Your room looks much like mine."

"Aye."

He wondered if she would change her mind, now that she knew what little he had. He almost wished she hadn't agreed to come with him. A refusal then would have been easier to stomach. Here she came like a vision come true, the only beauty he'd ever known, and to let her leave again would tear him in two.

He went to bar the door, and then thought

better of it. He felt as if he had walked into a trap of his own making, and yet had no notion of how it held him or any chance of escaping it.

"What worries you, *mon charmant*?" she asked.

He had the strength of a hundred men, and had bedded dozens of females. He knew almost as much about facking as he did trapping. Yet in another moment his knees would start to shake, or he would run from her.

Desperately he seized on an excuse to leave her so he could better compose himself. "You had naught to eat tonight. I'll fetch something from the kitchens."

"I'm not hungry for food." She came to stand beside him, and touched the bolt bar, running her fingertips against it before she dropped it in place. "You said you want me in your bed. Now that we are here, you are not sure. What has changed?"

"Naught." Broden knew if he touched her he wouldn't stop, so he went to his bench, and sat down to remove his boots. "'Tis much you dinnae ken of me."

"Oh?" She turned and leaned against the door. "Tell me this much."

In that moment he would have given anything to be one of the other hunters. Broden had long ago accepted what he was, but that didn't make it any easier to admit.

"I'm no' Mag Raith by blood," he told her. "Another tribe's headman got me on his bed slave. 'Twas from she my looks came."

Mariena seemed unmoved when he looked up at her. "She must have been magnificent, your mother."

"I've no memory of her in truth." Barefoot, he rose and unlaced the front of his tunic. "She died birthing me."

Now pity softened her expression. "I am sorry that you never knew her."

Broden didn't want her sympathy, but what more could she offer? He'd lived a paltry life on the fringes of a tribe not his own. His sire had given him nothing, and had laughed at the one lass who had offered to become his mate. Even being taken by the Sluath hadn't changed his circumstances. He'd done nothing but survive since the day he'd been born, and even that had largely been by chance. Had his sire not found Sileas trying to squeeze the life out of him, he would have rotted away long ago alongside his mother in her unmarked grave.

He should tell her that, so she would see what he was.

"This"—he touched the old scar on his throat—"came from my sire's mate, Sileas. After my *máthair* died she didnae wish to raise a slave's brat, so she made to strangle me. 'Twas what ruined my voice, and compelled my sire send me to be raised among the Mag Raith."

Her expression darkened, and she muttered something that sounded vicious under her breath.

"Domnall's tribe treated me well enough, but among the Pritani I held no rank or property. Most of the females desired me, but none would choose me as mate. I didnae ken why until much later, when my sire's mate made it plain to me." He pulled his tunic up over his head and tossed the garment on the bench. "The Sluath couldnae enslave me. I came to them a slave. I've been thus since my birth. 'Tis my only legacy."

Her lips thinned, and her jaw set. "The others, they consider you a slave?"

"No, my lady. The Mag Raith regard me as a brother, as do I them." He reached back for the laces of his trews, but stopped as she approached him. "I tell you so you will ken I've naught to offer you but my pretty face, and what see you here."

Mariena frowned as she halted. "This is why you scowl? All I can remember of my life is that I was a slave of the Sluath. I dropped into this time with nothing, not even clothes. What is it you think I have to offer you?"

He hadn't expected her to see them as equals. "'Tis that you deserve better, my lady, than a slaveborn lover who may give you naught."

"Pah. I want only you, and you are here." She stepped closer, until only an inch separated them. "Jenna told me why she and Rosealise were taken, to be used by their men for sex. I feel nothing for Kiaran, and my marks are the same as yours, so I think the Sluath took me to be your slave." She watched his eyes. "Ah, this is why you are so careful. This is what you desire, no?"

A stream of dark yearning jolted through him, but he shook his head. "Never would I think you my bed slave."

"Very good. This is how I feel, too. I would rather be your lover again." Mariena tore open the front of her shift, pushing it down to her waist until it dropped around her ankles. She stepped out of it, and then knelt naked at his feet. "Only I cannot remember what pleases you."

To see her like that made his blood run

molten and his cock swell to a painful stiffness. "You please me, my lady."

"I will." Her breasts rose and fell with her quickened breaths. "But you must tell me what to do, Broden."

❧

MARIENA WATCHED as a change came over Broden, the anguish fading from his expression. His eyes grew so dark they looked black now, and the bulge beneath the front of his trousers grew larger. Sweat shone on his temples and across his brow, and made a sheen across the muscular vault of his chest.

This was exactly what he wanted.

She'd sensed this need of his before, when she'd told him he'd nearly enslaved her with a kiss. He'd tried to hide his reaction, but she'd seen how it had affected him. It made perfect sense to her, too. Broden might look like a god, but he'd been treated as less than human. After nearly being killed for simply having been born, he'd been sent away from his people. He'd had no status among the Mag Raith, and only friendship with the other men. With his physical beauty he'd probably been subjected to the desires of others all his life, but always denied his own.

Giving him this control now could be the first time in his life he'd had it.

What he wanted echoed inside Mariena as well, in a new and incredible revelation. She was not placating him. She wanted this for herself, too. She was so tired of always being so restrained and watchful and guarded. Her answering excitement made her nipples pucker and her sex flower, pulsing with liquescent need. Surrendering her will to his made her feel oddly even more powerful.

"You wish me to command you," he finally said. "As a master would a bed slave." He tried to keep the longing from his voice, but his eyes told her that was exactly what he wished.

"Yes. I will not call you master, but yes."

"You would give yourself over to me." He didn't move or try to touch her, and she knew he wanted her to be sure. "To do as I say. Willingly."

Broden spoke as if this were a dangerous thing. Because they were strangers Mariena knew that it could be. She had been truthful. She knew nothing of how he was as a lover, or what particularly gave him pleasure. She wanted to know, and perhaps that element of risk was what made her desire it. Mariena didn't care what compelled her. In some part of her she simply knew it was how it should be between them.

"I will." Her heart pounded so frantically she could feel it shaking her breasts. "That is what I want."

"Then take off my trews, my lady," Broden said, his rasping voice going soft.

Her hands shook as she reached behind him and tugged at the laces there before slipping the trousers down his hips and thighs to his knees. Slowly she removed the garment, folded it neatly and placed it on the floor next to her. Her hair spilled down her back as she looked up at him.

He towered over her like the god he resembled, his dark hair falling around the perfection of his face. His body appeared flawless but for the old scar on his throat, tall and powerful, sleek muscles sculpted by his darkly tanned skin. No woman could have looked at him naked and not wanted to touch. Mariena wondered if she had the strength to resist all the temptations of his physical beauty.

"Clasp your hands behind your back." As she did so her breasts rose higher, as if she were shamelessly presenting them for his approval. She had never liked the tattoos the Sluath had inked over her shoulder and breast, but seeing his so close to her own made her fiercely glad they had marked her for him.

He reached down to cup her face, and looked into her eyes as he rubbed his thumb across her mouth. “Gods, but you’re so lovely.”

Broden made her feel that way. He traced her cheekbones and brows before returning his hand to her mouth. He seemed fascinated by her too-full lips. In a subtle invitation Mariena parted them for him, and he pushed inside to stroke the tip of her tongue slowly. She closed over him and sucked lightly, and felt his fingers tighten on her jaw. She wanted to do this to that thick, hard column springing from the black curls between his thighs, to rub him with her tongue as she took him deep. He would thrust between her lips as he did now, and watch her sucking his cock with his hot black eyes unblinking. She would take every inch of him into her, if he would allow it.

To be completely controlled by his desires felt incredibly freeing. All she had to do was yield herself to his passion, and let him show her the way to please him. How could she not remember this about herself?

Because I was this way only with him.

Broden took his thumb from her mouth, making her go still, and pushed his fingers into her hair at the back of her head. With his other hand he grasped his shaft, and brought the engorged head to her lips. "Put your mouth on my cock, lass."

She suspected he was testing her now, to see if she would be repelled by such a flagrantly intimate act. How could he doubt her still? She hesitated, closing her eyes for a moment, and felt his grip on her hair loosen. Bathing him first with a sigh, she opened and took his cockhead between her lips. His flesh felt hot and tight, a dome of satin from which she tasted a trace of seed. She sought more of that with her tongue, laving the eye of him gently, loving the fullness in her mouth as much as the taste of him.

Pushing in a little deeper, Broden uttered a low groan.

Tugging on him gently, Mariena silently begged him for more. She wanted him to penetrate deeper, to ravish her mouth with every inch of his hard, proud penis. She sucked and tongued and caressed him with her lips, moving her head now as she impaled her mouth on him. He guided her with his hand, urging her forward until the tip of her nose grazed his belly and his cock slid into her to his root.

He was so swollen and long she wondered if she would choke on his girth, but then she tilted her head and was able to take his pumping thrusts without difficulty. She felt as if she had been made for this, her wide mouth and full lips perfectly suited to pleasure him in this fashion. What startled her was how much it aroused her to submit to his thorough pillaging. She could feel her own wetness on her thighs, and the knot of her clit bulging and throbbing so madly she might come with his big cock still plunging in and out of her lips.

Broden drew all the way from her mouth, and bent down to take hold of her. He hauled her up in his hands and carried her over to the bed, pushing her down on her back before he straightened. He wasn't rough, but neither was he careful, and when he looked down at her his hands clenched at his sides.

The weight of his gaze alone made her sex ache for him.

Mariena watched the glistening shaft jutting from his body, and parted her thighs just as she had her lips. *Come, touch me, take me,* she pleaded silently.

Broden didn't move, so she spread her legs a little more. She knew he could see what he had done to her, and it added to the torment of waiting and watching him. She had no idea of what he would do to her, or what he would ask of her. That, too, excited her beyond all measure.

The ticking crackled under her as Broden climbed onto the bed. Without ceremony he straddled her like some huge dark beast pouncing on helpless prey. Everywhere his skin met hers, it prickled with nerves. The stark contrast of his hard, dark body against the softer, pallid gleam of hers made her think of moonlight glowing against the night sky.

He took hold of her wrists and drew her arms up over her head, pinning her hands to the ticking. "Remain thus."

As he drew back his muscular thighs tightened against her hips, and he looked down at her arching breasts with hooded eyes. Slowly his hands encircled her curves, holding and then fondling her with maddening gentleness. His touch made her catch her lower lip between her teeth, but even that could not prevent the whimper of wanting that came from her.

"Your mouth on me nearly made me spill on your tongue," he told her as he plucked at her aching peaks. "Another time I shall, and watch you swallow my cream, and lick it from your lips. But I reckon you want my cock in your wet little quim. You ache for me now, dinnae you?"

"Yes." The word burst from her shivering in the air.

"'Tis my desires you wish to serve," he chided.

Even his teasing aroused her. "But this is how you make me feel, *mon ange*. Is that not what you want?"

"'Tis only what I've dreamt." That came out in a rumble, as if something inside him were breaking.

One of his hands stroked down over her belly, curving over the pale down covering her sex as if petting her there. His long fingers parted her folds, one grazing over the full pearl of her clit before rimming the ellipse of her opening beneath it. He played with her there for a long moment as he watched her face, and then sank his finger into her, sliding it deep before drawing it out again.

Still holding her gaze, he brought his hand to his mouth, and tasted her wetness.

It was too much, Mariena thought, trembling as she struggled to remain as he wanted her. Would he go on tormenting her like this for the rest of the night? Could she bear it if he did? This was not so much surrender as a test of wills—hers against his. He would do his best to arouse her to shrieking, quivering helplessness, but somehow she would bear it and instead serve his yearning for her acquiescence.

Broden's hands took hold of her thighs, and pushed them up as he settled between them. He notched his shaft against her folds, moving his hips as he rubbed his length against that slick, heated seam. Instead of entering her, he moved back. His hands shifted around her knees, and then under them as he positioned her legs even higher, and gazed at what that revealed of her. His expression shifted again, this time to that of a man discovering a precious treasure.

"'Tis only for this night?" he asked her, biting out the words.

It took her a moment to work out what he meant. "If you wish." She wanted more, but this was about what he desired.

His dark eyes burned into hers, and then he seemed to read her mind. "You shall tell me *your* desire, my lady."

"You." She stretched a little, knowing he would follow the movement with his gaze, wanting his eyes on her. "I'd be with you every night like this."

"'Tis the same for me," he told her, his shoulders stiff as he braced himself over her. "Come to my chamber, and you shall have me—no. We shall have each other."

"Yes," Mariena moaned the word as she felt him coming into her, his fist guiding his thick cockhead to her folds, and pushing it into her wetness.

The passionate, heart-rending kiss they'd shared in her room had prepared her for this, or so she thought. As he penetrated her Mariena became suffused in so many sensations she thought her body would burst with them. Broden bent down to take her mouth with his, and claimed it with his tongue just as he filled her with his cock. Being taken in both ways made her whole body shake. Would she come apart under him, her body unable to withstand the slamming waves of their desires colliding, or could she take all of his ravenous hunger?

He ended that consuming kiss, and lifted his head to look into her eyes as he slowly moved against her. The slide of his penis out of her clinging softness made her swallow a cry that escaped her as soon as he plunged back inside her. She gripped the ticking now, trying to brace herself for his thrusts, but he took over her body as surely as he had her self-control.

"Mariena," he said through his teeth, and when she stared up at him he pressed higher, fucking her so hard and fast the bed slammed into the stone wall behind it.

All thought left her as she gave in to the glorious beast he had become, and the primal delight of accepting his rough passion. Even with his great strength he would never harm her, she knew that without a doubt. With her own strength she answered his, countering every thrust with her hips, taking him deeper, urging him on. Inside her she felt her own pleasure coming together, thick and heavy, and ruthlessly resisted it.

This time was for him. She was his, and she would give him what he wanted.

Broden came into her and went rigid as his

cock jerked. She clenched around him, squeezing him as he began to jet into her core, taking his seed from him with every pulse. He looked down at her, showing her the bliss taking him over, and that set her free. She arched under him as her own pleasure erupted, flinging hot delight through every part of her, and let him see it take her.

At last.

When the last tremors shook them both, Mariena felt the shadows inside her crumbling away and reforming into something made of the same dark light she saw in his eyes. She would never be who she had been before making love with this beautiful man. What would she become now that they had found each other again?

Broden reached for her hands, his tattooed arm brushing across her marked breast, and suddenly they both fell through his bed onto white-blue sands.

Chapter Fourteen

AS BRODEN RAN after Mariena in the underworld arena, he glanced at the rounded tiers of stone that surrounded them, each holding strange bars where the Sluath would perch like vultures to watch the slaves battle. All of their roosts stood empty now, so perhaps he could leave this wretched place without spilling her blood.

He had never fought a female in his life, and yet her determination to escape had forced him to come to this gruesome place, to do that very thing. For that he hated her.

Mariena's thin gown fluttered around her, the fabric so fine it looked almost transparent here in the glaring lights. Nimbly she crossed the sands, leaping over the piles of bleached bone left by the old battles, and splashes of bloody gore from the new. The effort of chasing her tugged at the many thin wounds on his back, causing some of them to break open. He stopped when she found no avenue of escape and turned to face him.

The harsh, over-bright light seemed to soften as it touched her. She looked like a queen with her hair piled atop her head, and the pale gold pearls they had woven through the coils.

Seeing the wintry colors of her so fully illuminated made Broden remember the moment he'd first been mesmerized by Mariena's frosty beauty. Seabhag had delivered her like a sack of grain, dragging her by the blood-stained collar of her gown to fling her unconscious body at his feet. She'd been dressed in a torn drab gown, and some sort of fine clay coated her face. Dark bruises covered her arms, and raw cord marks braceleted her wrists.

It enraged him to see the abuse she'd suffered, but in this place he had learned to hold back his fury. The demons liked to use it to hurt other mortals. They'd even made him beat Mael once while the other Sluath had watched.

"A gift for you, Pritani." The Sluath's smile

shifted along with his visage, from the grin of a stripling to the smirk of a toothless hag.

"Why should I want an ugly, broken female?" Broden countered, scowling.

"If I have to explain that to you"—the demon nudged her over onto her back—"then you are not the mortal I thought you. Under that makeup she's not so ugly, either."

He inspected her limp body. "Why gift her to me?"

"Why not? You've been an obedient boy lately, and I'm feeling generous." Seabhag changed into a tall, slender druid in white robes. "She'll be your slave until I return from the next culling. You may do anything you like to her—anything—and no one will stop you. There won't be another, however, so try not to kill her too quickly."

As soon as they had been left alone Mariena had opened her eyes, pushed herself to her feet and run from him. Darting around his chamber, she frantically searched for something. Only after she tried to shatter one of the unbreakable pitchers and then held it like a cudgel did Broden understand she wanted a weapon.

She had made him understand many things since that moment.

Her fearlessness would be her end, Broden thought now as he felt more blood running down his back. She'd already attacked two guards, and she would do the same to any demon who came near her now. If they were caught outside the chamber Mariena would be dragged off to the punishment post, and he made to watch her being whipped. The Sluath particularly enjoyed brutalizing beauties. They would crowd around to enjoy her pain as she writhed and bled.

Yet if they learned why she'd escaped the chamber this time they would torture and then kill her. They might even make him end her.

"You think you can put your hands on me, and I will do nothing?" Mariena shouted as she kicked sand at him, her face taut with fury. "I'll never spread my legs for a demon."

"I told ye, I'm no' Sluath." He let all the anger he felt flood through him. "Ye're my slave now, wench. Accept your fate."

Two swords came hurling out of the shadows, landing hilts up in the white-blue sands. He bent down to seize them, and tossed one to her. She caught it easily and backed away, holding it ready. When their eyes met he saw in them her unwavering determination.

Icy sweat broke out on his brow. She would not go without a fight.

"The only thing you'll put in my belly, Pritani, is that blade," Mariena said as she circled, keeping her back to the stone tiers.

Out of the corner of his eye Broden saw the small, bairn-like demon Meirneal appear alongside Seabhag, whose body shimmered as he shifted from the form of a slender boy to that of an ancient man. Both were as vicious as the rest of the demons, but Meirneal had a taste for flawless young flesh. The moment he saw Mariena he would want to sink his sharp little teeth into her.

That left Broden with no choice but to run at her.

Just before he came within striking distance Mariena flung sand into his face. Blinded, he reeled back, and heard the hiss of her weapon through the air. He spun, but not in time to avoid the slash of her blade across his chest. He lunged, using a quick thrust of his elbow to knock her on her back. As she pushed herself up he kicked the sword out of her hand.

She straightened and met his gaze, her eyes blazing with emotion, and then screamed as she pounced on him.

Broden shook her off, back-handing her as she tried to leap on him a second time. She staggered and fell heavily on her front. When she lifted her face, choking out a mouthful of sand, he pressed his boot to her neck.

"'Tis done," he told her harshly. "Stay down."

He turned to see the demons watching them with great interest, and hurled his sword at them. With his claws Seabhag batted away the blade as if it were no more than a twig. When it fell to the sands it crumbled into pebbles of their strange stone.

"Ye didnae say she'd fight me," he told Seabhag as he snatched Mariena up and clamped her arms behind her back. When she tried to bite his arm, he used one hand to grab her by the hair and hold her face away from him. "'Tis all she does."

"What fun would you have if she were willing?" the demon replied. "I think you've relied too long on that pretty face to do the work for you. Beat her into submission. That always works with her type."

Broden could hardly speak for the hatred welling up in him, but this was his chance to obtain what he needed. "If I'm to keep her in my chamber ye must give me shackles and chains. Once she's proper bound I can fack her until she stops fighting me."

Mariena began to swear in her native tongue as she struggled even more violently against his hold.

"I will see to it at once," the shifting demon said, his tone pleased.

"Just a moment." The sweet-faced Meirneal trod over to them, wrinkling his tiny nose with distaste as he passed the splashes of blood and gore on the sands. He took out a square of fine cloth edged in lace and held it over his nose as he stopped in front of Mariena, inspecting her closely. "Hmm."

"What now?" the other demon asked.

"All here is not what it seems." He took away the cloth and breathed in deeply. "Can't you smell it? This female fairly reeks of treachery."

Broden tensed. He knew he couldn't hurt the demon, and he had no weapon now anyway.

"She's had that smell since I culled her from that lovely spot in Paris. Such a scrumptious little torture chamber. She seemed to be enjoying herself immensely right before I took her." Seabhag's body reformed itself into a duplicate of

Mariena's as he joined them. "You know, with the life she led in the mortal realm, she could make an interesting diversion for our prince."

"Then take *him* the chains and shackles," Broden suggested, "for she's as a wounded animal, and wants naught of any male."

"Oh, yes, please," she begged, grinning widely. "Give me to your prince. I will whore myself for anyone but this pig Pritani."

"How endearing." Meirneal looked intrigued now. "Tell me, are you especially fond of that tongue?"

"A willing concubine," Seabhag said. "No, I think not." He turned to Meirneal. "And you have mutilated enough slaves from this culling already, little fiend." The demon sighed before he regarded Broden. "I'll send a guard with restraints. Go back to your cell." He made a shooing gesture with a hand that shifted from a gnarled claw to a wet flipper.

"Do you hear that, wench? Ye'll no' run from me again." Broden jerked her away.

The small demon chuckled. "Don't use her too much, Pritani. Save something for the culling feast. As pretty as you are, I expect our prince to want you to perform as part of the slave spectacle. Now, Seabhag, I would consult with you on that hulking one I've marked. Do you think a female of comparable size would present the right incentive, or should I cull something much smaller?"

"The larger females do last longer," the shifting demon said as they walked back to the tunnel between the tiers. "If you do not play with them first, of course."

Broden dragged Mariena toward the entry to the slave tunnels, gritting his teeth as she fought him with all her strength. "Be still, wench, or I shall fack ye here while they watch us."

❧

THE GLARING LIGHT FADED, and the arena sands darkened and hardened into stone. Mariena came out of the memory and froze as she looked into Broden's narrowed eyes. They stood naked in the middle of his room, and she held something long and heavy. When she looked down she had his sword in her hand, her arm drawn back and the tip poised to thrust into his belly. He was holding his dagger to her throat.

Mariena blinked, unsure of what to do. They

had just made love, but somehow now they stood prepared to kill each other.

"Dinnae move, my lady." Moving very slowly and deliberately, he took away the blade, throwing the weapon behind him as he stepped back from her. "I didnae intend to do this. A vision bespelled me."

"You and I fought in the demon's arena," Mariena said. "I saw it." Slowly, she lowered the sword and let it drop. She had been clutching it so tightly her fingers felt bruised.

Wordlessly Broden pulled on his trews, and brought her shift to her. She stared at it for a moment as she recalled the dress she had worn in the arena, and lifted a hand to touch her hair. They had dressed and adorned her like that—for him—but that meant nothing. He'd said horrible things to her and the demons. Thinking about it made her head feel as if someone were beating on it with a hammer.

"My lady."

She looked at him, and saw the torment in her heart reflected in his eyes. "*Bon sang*. I might have killed you."

"I wish you had." Broden sounded sincere,

and badly shaken. "What I did to you…'tis beyond shameful."

"It cannot be true," Mariena said and pulled on her shift as she thought about it. "In dreams such things happen. We might have fallen asleep, and that is what we shared." But how could that be possible?

"I've dreamt of you for weeks, my lady." He shook his head. "We never fought. I reckoned them memories of you." His mouth thinned. "Now I think no'."

"This could be the work of the demons, to make us think we were enemies." As she reached out to him he moved back, startling her. "Broden, I will not hurt you, I promise."

"Our skinwork touched just before the vision." He held his inked arm away from her. "I'll no' risk another."

"No, wait, we should do it again." She wasn't afraid of him, and if he were a threat, she would be. "We may recall more. I want to know why we were fighting in the arena."

"We returned from the vision armed and poised to strike each other." Broden shook his head. "I'll no' risk harming you to remember how we suffered in that facking place."

"It does not matter that I cannot remember the reason for the fight. You could never hurt a woman in anger, *mon charmant*," she assured him. "That I know. It isn't in you."

He stiffened as she said that, and drew back from her. "I shall take you back to your chamber."

Chapter Fifteen

AS DAWN LIGHTENED the great hall, Domnall set the bundle of firewood down by the hearth, and heard someone moving in the kitchens. Drawing his dagger, he soundlessly approached the entry, only to sheathe the blade when he saw the source of the noise.

Edane stood behind Kiaran, who sat with his arms braced on Rosealise's work table. In front of them sat the archer's box of medicines beside some wide swaths of dark red-crusted linen. The falconer's pale, drawn face and shadowed eyes spoke of suffering, and his knotted fists of pain.

"I thought your wounds healed," Domnall said as he joined them, and then saw the blackened lesions and smears of dried blood on his back. "By the Gods, what did this?"

"A sword wielded blindly," Kiaran said, hissing in reaction as Edane applied a thick, odorous salve to the burns. "I dinnae recommend the method."

"'Twas no' my doing, Chieftain," the shaman said, his disgust plain. "In the night our canny brother here thought it wise to hack off his new flesh." He thumped down the pot of salve. "Happily, he well-heated the blade first, or I reckon we'd be digging his grave now."

Kiaran sighed. "We're immortal, Brother."

"Then why bled you half the night? Why havenae the burns closed and healed?" Edane countered before he glanced at Domnall. "'Tis like the gash on Broden's throat. It seems we dinnae recover as quickly as once we did. I cannae fathom why."

After more than a thousand years of the Mag Raith living free of sickness and injury, this new development boded nothing good.

"Why didnae you come to us?" Domnall asked the falconer.

"Would you have done thus?" When he shook

his head Kiaran smiled. "You've your answer, Chieftain."

Broden then came into the kitchens, and the trapper looked almost as sickly as the falconer.

"I'm to collect my snares from the woods, for we've enough game to last until the next moon," he said to Domnall. "Tell Mael I'll take the tower boundary patrol for him today as well. Edane, will you watch after Mistress Douet?"

"Aye, once I've finished with our idiot brother here." He took up some clean linen and began to tear it into strips, but when he regarded the trapper he frowned. "Your neck, 'tis healed. When did the wound close?"

"The morning after the battle." Broden looked at Kiaran, flinched, and then swore under his breath as he stalked out.

Domnall knew the trapper to be in no mood to confide his reasons for taking on the additional watch, so he focused on Kiaran. "We're immortal, Brother, no' imperishable. I ken this new affliction caused you anguish, but you took too great a risk."

"You reckon I'd wait to become as the Sluath?" the falconer asked softly.

The fresh bandages dropped from Edane's hands. "Brother, no."

"'Tis no telling what horror I might inflict as a demon amongst the clan," Kiaran told him. "Should I lose what's left of my soul and become that, I'd turn against you. Could you even stop me?"

"We would," Domnall assured him gently, seeing now the true cause of his pain. "Never doubt that, Brother. I'd spare you damnation."

He nodded, and some of the lines around his mouth eased.

"You dinnae ken 'twould happen thus," Edane told him as he began winding the new bandages around his chest and back. "'Twas mayhap due to your power to see through your birds that Galan's spell to reverse your arrows changed your body. Or didnae you reckon that while planning this mutilation?"

"I couldnae think beyond being rid of the damned wings," Kiaran admitted, his shoulders slumping.

Leaving the falconer to his self-imposed exile had been a mistake, Domnall thought. He also had to speak to Mariena about his new scheme, so he decided to tackle both at once.

"I want you returned to your chamber in the stronghold by nightfall," he told Kiaran. When he started to protest he added, "'Tisnae a request. You shall also invite Mistress Douet to see your forge after we break our fast."

Edane met his gaze and nodded. "'Tis a good day to show her the works."

Domnall later noticed Mariena watching the entries to the hall as the clan shared he morning meal, and suspected Broden's absence the cause of her vigil. Although she never spoke a great deal, she seemed especially quiet this morning, and ate only a little of Rosealise's excellent morning meal of spiced porridge, oat cakes and jam. While Kiaran joined them after changing into a clean tunic, and nodded to the French-woman, he barely touched his food as well.

"We've got trouble brewing," Jenna said to him in the kitchens as he helped her with clearing the table. "I just can't tell who's causing it: Broden, Mariena, or Kiaran." She eyed him. "I'm guessing you do."

"Aye, but leave them to me." He brushed his mouth over hers. "'Tis time I stopped coddling our difficult bairns."

"You mean our problem children," she said

before she kissed him back. "Be kind to them anyway. It usually works better than yelling and punching. If you need me I'll be thatching the east passage roof with Mael today."

He returned to the great hall in time to hear Kiaran ask the Frenchwoman if she would care to see his workplace. She seemed surprised by the invitation, but nodded her agreement.

"I'll accompany you, Mistress Douet," Domnall said. "I'd welcome your reckoning on a new blade our smith makes."

WALKING with Kiaran and the chieftain to the forge gave Mariena a little time to consider why they wanted her there. Not to inspect a weapon, although it seemed a good excuse. She felt certain they did not know about her being intimate with Broden. As men they would have looked at her differently. As for the vision she'd shared with him, she doubted he would tell anyone about it, either. This had something to do with her, not her affair with their trapper.

Not that their *coup d'un soir* qualified as even a brief affair.

It had shocked her when Broden had marched her back to her chamber and left without another word. After what they had shared together she couldn't understand it. His absence at the morning meal made it plain that he was going to avoid her now. Either he regretted the encounter, or still felt shame over what he had done to her in the vision of their underworld battle. Regardless of Broden's reasons for rejecting and avoiding her, Mariena felt sure the vision could not be the truth of what had really happened between them in the slave arena.

It seemed as wrong as Broden taking her back to her room.

At the end of a long passage the men stopped, and Domnall opened two heavy doors lined on the inside with plated bronze.

"Kiaran rebuilt the castle's forge just after we came to Dun Chaill. During our mortal lives he worked for our tribe's smith," the chieftain said as he led her inside. "He recalled enough to repair the stonework and fashion the proper tools."

The falconer lit some lamps to illuminate the dark work room, which looked only a little larger than Mariena's own chamber. Buckets of water had been placed all around the wide, scarred work table off to one side. Cooler air came in as Domnall removed a shutter from a narrow window. That and some large vent shafts in the ceiling helped dispel the strong smells of woodsmoke and heated metal. In front of the enormous stone hearth sat a wide anvil atop a large tree stump, against which a long pair of metal tongs leaned. Racks of hammers of different shapes flanked the forge. So did long rows of finished swords, daggers and spear heads.

The fact that Mariena liked being surrounded by so many lethal weapons only gave her a little pang of worry. Perhaps she had worked for a butcher—and suddenly pain shot through her worry. She had to stop wondering why things were like this for her.

The falconer took down a heavy, full-length leather apron and offered it to her. "'Twill protect your garments, my lady."

She nodded and slipped the neck strap over her head, and then watched him fire the huge stone hearth against the back wall. The way Kiaran moved suggested he was in pain, and she could see some spots of blood on the back of his tunic. She'd never felt a need to use her healing power, but now her fingers itched with the urge to touch him.

I cannot do this in front of the chieftain. He'll see the wound transfer to my body. Something brushed her arm and in a panic she jerked away.

"Forgive me, my lady," Domnall said, holding up the hand he'd used to touch her. "Feel you unwell?"

"No, not at all." Her whole face had flushed, Mariena realized, and pressed the back of her hand to her cheek. "This apron, it is a little warm."

"'Twill grow hotter," Kiaran warned as he tugged on a rope hanging beside the forge. Flames and sparks flared up from a wide bed of charcoal before he donned padded leather gloves, and tugged a kind of hatch across the front of the hearth. "When I finish for the day I must soak my broiling hide in the river."

But not today, Mariena thought, glancing at the rigid way he held his shoulders as he tied another leather apron over himself. Had he fallen in that tower where he liked to hide? If he'd landed on his shoulders, that might explain the injuries.

While Kiaran took down several hammers she glanced at the chieftain. "It is very interesting, this place, but you did not bring me here to watch your man sweat or look at a blade. What did you truly wish to discuss?"

Domnall smiled a little. "Since we gathered in the greenhouse we've seen no signs of the watcher. I reckon he's found a way to eavesdrop on us there, so last night I bade Edane ward the forge."

"Oh, you are clever." She grinned. "He would never expect that."

"'Tis my hope, my lady." The chieftain beckoned for her to move back from the now-roaring forge. "We need find and deal with this bastart before he again strikes. Until we do, I'd ask your reckoning on how we might better protect our ladies from more attacks."

"They should be trained to better defend themselves. Also, to signal for help if they are in trouble, and you to signal them when an attack comes," she suggested. "Your hand signals only work when you are with them. Carve whistles for all of us to carry and use with coded sounds. I will work with them on how to fight." As he nodded, she thought about what he'd said. "You believe this watcher targets your women?"

The chieftain related the details of several

suspicious incidents involving his wife, Rosealise and Nellie. While he admitted he'd thought them at first to be accidents, the frequency and circumstances led him and the other men to believe the watcher wanted to kill each woman.

"As hunters we ken luring tactics," Domnall said. "With Jenna 'twas gems, and Lady Rosealise a map, but naught for Lady Nellie."

"Her power to touch-read would have exposed the watcher's intention," Mariena guessed. "For her he had to create a trap she could not escape."

"Aye, that seems his purpose," Kiaran said as he used the bronze tongs to draw back the forge hatch and place an old sword into the flames. "Only why wouldnae he persist with his attacks? A hunter doesnae give up after a trap fails. He builds another, else he starves."

Domnall thought for a moment. "The attacks ceased after Dun Chaill brought back each of our ladies from death."

Mariena couldn't agree with his assumption about the castle, but she suspected he'd found the reason why no more traps had been set.

"Broden told me that others have been murdered in these lands," Mariena said. "That could be the work of this watcher. The dead, they were all mortals, too, no?"

The chieftain nodded. "Yet why would the watcher no' wish mortals at Dun Chaill?"

"That you must ask him," Kiaran said as he drew the sword from the flames, and set it against the anvil. "Would you hold out your arm, my lady, that I may see your reach?"

Mariena did as he asked, and watched as he hammered a notch into the glowing blade. "You are cutting down this sword for me?"

"'Twill give you more control with less weight and span." The falconer positioned the notch at the end of the anvil and struck off a portion of the metal.

"If you mean to keep walking the walls at dawn," Domnall told her, "then you'll carry a weapon. I'll show you the spell barrier today so you ken its boundaries. If you ride, you may patrol the barrier with us. I'll fashion the whistles, but teach you our hand signals as well."

She hadn't tried to conceal her morning habit, but it pleased her that the chieftain had noticed her efforts. "You no longer wish to protect me as the helpless female?"

"Helpless?" His mouth hitched. "You're

strong, swift, and handle a blade as any of the Mag Raith would, my lady. Naught escapes your notice, and you've a particular knack for strategy. Our ladies arenae helpless, but they've no' your talents. I've but five sword arms to defend this stronghold. With you I'll have six."

For the first time since dropping from the sky into this time Mariena felt completely at ease.

"If that is the case, then I should like two daggers along with the sword, please. I also wish to search the interior of the stronghold. For that I will need the scroll map Rosealise found in her chamber." Before he could disagree she held up her hand. "I do not seek to open more traps. I wish to look for other signs of this watcher that have perhaps escaped you."

"'Tis good," Domnall said. "Now permit me teach you our signals."

Mariena had no trouble learning the basic gestures the hunters used to communicate without words. Since the Mag Raith used dozens the chieftain taught her those he thought she most needed to know, and promised to show her the remainder in the days ahead.

She frowned as she considered how scanty their numbers were. "Jenna told me most castles in this time have garrisons of soldiers to help defend it. There are no men close enough here to recruit as soldiers for Dun Chaill?"

"If we leave the barrier," Domnall said, "the Sluath shall ken. Galan and the Sluath destroyed the nearest village. The watcher also has attacked many mortals who stray too close to the castle."

The door to the forge opened, and Mael called to Domnall, who excused himself and went to speak with him.

Mariena went over to watch the falconer as he filed down the broken end of the blade. The urge to touch him had faded, and she saw the blood on the back of his shirt had already dried. He also seemed to be moving easier, which made her feel a little better about not healing him.

"You are very good at this work," she said. The way he plied the file intrigued her. "It is made of iron?"

"Aye, as all our weapons. Only that ends the demons." He glanced at her. "You neednae flatter me, my lady. I saw how 'twould be with you and our trapper the night of the battle."

She shrugged. "Lucky for you. I might have cut open *your* neck."

"Broden's the proudest, most mulish arse I've

ever ken. He's also as near to a true brother to me as if we shared blood," Kiaran said as he straightened and inspected the new tip. "You shouldnae trifle with him."

"I never trifle," Mariena told him calmly. "Why do you warn me? Has he spoken of me to you?"

The falconer only smiled as he took the shortened blade and thrust it back into the forge.

Domnall returned. "If you've seen your fill, my lady, I'd take you to the stables now."

As they went to the door a thought occurred to Mariena. Had the watcher been the cause of the vision she and Broden had shared? If he was half-Sluath, he might have the power to alter their dreams.

"A moment, please," she said to the chieftain as he reached for the latch. "If we are correct about the watcher not wishing mortals here at Dun Chaill, then certainly I will be his next target."

"'Tis likely, and another reason I want you armed," he admitted. "I'll no' see another lady harmed by this bastart."

"That is part of the problem, Monsieur. You wait for him to act, and he knows this. We must turn his tactics against him, and lure him to us. I could be the bait in a trap we set for him."

The chieftain regarded her for a long moment. "Aye. We should speak on it with Broden when he returns. For now, I must go and help Mael secure some new rafters before they fall on my lady's head."

"Of course," Mariena said. "Where did your trapper go? There is something else I wish to discuss with him."

Chapter Sixteen

GALAN REINED IN his horse as he reached the outskirts of the old druid settlement, and looked down at the young boy perched on the front of his saddle.

"You see, Druman? There 'tis, just as I vowed to you." He could see a few of the mortal spies he had summoned to attend him as well. They stood waiting and watching from the ruins. With a flick of power and thought he sent them to fetch firewood.

"'Tis taken hours and hours to reach this place," the little boy said and sighed. "I'm tired and thirsty, and I need to make water."

"Soon you shall rest, my lad," Galan told him as he spurred on the mount.

Luring the young druid away from the

Emerald Glen had been ridiculously simple. No one would deny Bhaltair Flen anything he wished. When he had proposed taking Druman for a ride the headman had immediately called it a fine idea. The druidess defender had eyed the bairn, started to speak and then looked away, obviously unhappy.

"You neednae worry, Sister, for I've much experience with bairns," Galan had assured her. "'Twill be an adventure he'll no' soon forget. What do you say, lad?"

Druman nodded vigorously. "Yes. I'll go with you."

The boy made no fuss at all about being taken on the lengthy jaunt. He had listened to Galan talk about the non-existent wonders of the place, as intent as a much older youth. As the sun climbed overhead, his small body began to slump back, and he'd even fallen asleep for a time.

Once among the ruins of the settlement Galan clamped his arm around the lad and dismounted. Setting Druman on his feet, he hobbled his horse and took from his satchel a waterskin, from which he drank. When Galan did not offer the boy the skin, he opened the front of his small robes. A stream of urine came from him, narrowly missing Galan's boots.

"What do you?" he demanded, stepping back quickly.

"I make water." Druman calmly finished emptying his bladder before peering up at him. "You arenae nice."

"I'm head of the druid conclave," Galan told him. "I dinnae have to be."

The boy pursed his lips and then nodded, as if he'd said something wise. "Why do you bring me here?"

"I would ken the details of a chronicle you wrote in a previous incarnation. 'Twas that of the disappearance of the five Mag Raith hunters and their tribe." He waited for the lad to react. "You have lived many lives, Druman. I ken you recall each."

Now the boy would deny it, and Galan could finally begin to enjoy himself. He thought he would first beat Druman, and then compel him to lick his boots–

"You speak of my third life," the child said as if he were an adult. "I remember that one perfectly."

Galan hung his waterskin out of the lad's

reach on a tree. "Tell me everything you learned of the Mag Raith, and I shall give you all the drink you want."

Druman's tiny white teeth flashed. "If you dinnae attend to my body's needs, it shall become overwrought and no' allow me to speak. It shall revert to a bairn, then wail and weep until 'tis satisfied."

"Prove to me that you recollect what I'd ken," he countered.

"'Twas in the month before the Romans came from the south to hunt our kind that all of the Mag Raith vanished," the archivist said. "The first five set out on a hunt from which they never returned. Their tribe later journeyed in search of them, only to vanish as well."

Rapt now, Galan leaned closer. "Aye. Now, where went the hunters, and what was said of their fate?"

"No' far from this settlement," Druman said and pointed to the east. "Other Pritani claimed the invaders killed them, but none ever found their bodies. Nor those of their tribe. "'Twas said they had followed the five's trail into oblivion."

He watched the lad's ancient eyes. "'Twas your reckoning?"

"No." He bunched his small hands. "Too many gone. I came to the ridges, where I discovered…"

"What found you, Archivist?" Galan demanded.

Druman released a terrible screech, threw himself to the ground and began kicking his legs as he screamed in the bairn's voice, "Thirsty, hungry, want water, want food, now."

The lad's tantrum went on without any promise of soon ending. Although the temptation to beat Druman sorely needled Galan, such was his anger that he would likely end the bairn. He could not wait until the archivist reincarnated again, nor would he give reason for the Emerald Glen to blame Bhaltair Flen for the child's death. That would lead the real Flen directly to Galan.

He would have to coddle the tiny brat.

"Very well, you shall have both," he said, raising his voice to be heard, and then went to his horse to retrieve what food he'd brought for the journey. The child's continued screaming caused his mount to shuffle nervously and kick the hobbled leg at Galan. "Be still, you stupit nag."

Taking his satchel from the saddle loop, he turned as Druman stopped screeching. Yet the young druid no longer lay on the ground, or stood anywhere in sight. He dropped the pack and ran toward the spot, eyeing the dirt for tracks. The child had left behind only a crystal still flickering with power. It shattered the moment Galan tried to touch it, releasing one last bairn's screech as it pelted his face. The sense of someone approaching him from behind made him summon his power and spin.

An unfamiliar crofter stopped a short distance away, and shimmered as he shed the mortal illusion and took on a less constant shape.

"There you are, Druid," Seabhag said, frowning with three different mouths in succession. "What are you doing out here? Reliving your youth or abusing another's?"

Chapter Seventeen

COLLECTING HIS SNARES gave Broden welcome solitude and silence, but no peace. He shouldn't have left the stronghold, not after seeing Kiaran's wounds. His need to avoid Mariena had been so pressing that he'd ignored his brother's pain and imprudence. Still, with a glance he knew what the falconer had done. Although it sickened him, he also understood why Kiaran had wished to maim himself. He still could not look at his own hands without remembering how he'd hurt the woman of his dreams.

That he had remembered it immediately after taking Mariena as his lover made it only more agonizing.

After he retrieved the last of his snares he

would stow them in the stables and go out on patrol, but he couldn't ride the boundary forever. When he returned for the evening meal he would have to face Mariena again. Never had he been a coward, but he'd rather take a blade to his gut than sit near her and eat in silence. Yet what could he say?

Tell her the truth you've hidden all these centuries, Sileas's voice said behind his eyes. *Tell them what you meant to do after the final hunt. How your scheming forever damned the Mag Raith.*

His sire's mate had been so evil she'd tried to murder an infant, so Broden felt no particular obligation to do as her memory urged. His long life with his four brothers had also taught him that time could also bring some peace to the darkest heart. He'd ever tried in his own fashion to make amends for what he had inflicted on the Mag Raith.

Perhaps that I should do the same for Mariena. But how may I recompense for the suffering I caused her?

Broden walked to the blaeberry thicket where he'd left two rabbit snares, now entangled with a patch of unfamiliar, clustered white flowers on thick stalks. As he drew his dagger he frowned, for he hadn't noticed any new shoots when he'd set them. He'd probably been thinking about her, as he had every moment since she'd fallen from the sky.

"Do you decorate all your traps?" a voice he didn't want to hear asked.

Broden glanced over his shoulder to make sure he hadn't heard her in his head, and saw Mariena walking along the trail leading back toward Dun Chaill. She looked like a wraith against the dappled greens and browns of the forest, but as she drew nearer she passed through sunbeams that spilled a rosy glow over her pale skin and hair.

The light loved her as much as Broden wished he could.

"You do not have to speak to me, you know," Mariena assured him as she stopped and braced herself against the striped bark of a silver birch. "But when you look at me in that way, *mon ange*, it makes me want to take off my dress."

"Keep on your gown, my lady."

"I think I will." She wrinkled her nose as she glanced around them. "I do not want to be naked out here with you. With how we are together, we will get very dirty."

She thought this amusing? "You shouldnae be here alone with me."

"Pah. I am not afraid of you." Her lips curved. "Ah, I see. You fear you will hit me again, as you did in the vision. That is why you made me leave you last night."

"No," Broden bit out.

"You cannot control yourself." She threw up her hands. "You are a hopeless woman-beater."

"I've never beaten…" *a female other than you,* his heart taunted. "Return to the stronghold, my lady. 'Tis naught for you here."

"You are wrong. I like berries." Mariena pushed herself away from the birch. "Not as much as the taste of you, but I will settle."

"Willnae you listen?" Broden demanded, striding toward her. He was reaching for her shoulders, and then he remembered the vision and snatched his hands back. "I cannae protect you. I cannae have you."

Her amusement faded. "You had me last night. You promised me every night. I want that, Broden. I want you. Give me what I want, or there will be more of this, every day. In front of the clan."

He shook his head as he turned away from

her. "Leave me alone, my lady, before I hurt you again." He felt her following him. "I beg you."

Broden crouched down and reached in to cut the snares, triggering one that suddenly exploded. As sharp shards of wood flew through the air, the white flowers lashed against his face. Fire filled his eyes as he threw out his arm to keep her back, and then he fell to his knees as he clawed away the blooms.

"Broden?" She hissed with pain. "Ah, something hit my shoulder."

"Stay back," he told her, gritting his teeth as the burning pain spread. He closed his eyes and used his sleeve to wipe away the debris. As soon as he did agony exploded inside his head, and he fell back and bellowed.

Strong slender hands hooked under his arms, and Mariena dragged him back from the thicket. He heard her tearing cloth, and then felt her crouch down beside him and gently blot his face.

"What is it?" she asked, her hands shaking. "Why is your skin blistering?"

"'Tis the flowers." His roar of pain had reduced his gravelly voice to barely a rough whisper now. "They're poison. Dinnae touch me. Move away."

His fingers burned as he pulled off his tunic and threw it away from him, and then rubbed his hands in the soil. He looked to survey the damage, but only a mottled darkness filled his eyes.

"What can I do?" she asked, so close now her breath touched his mouth.

"Naught," he rasped. Broden felt the frantic thrum of her heart beat against the side of his arm as he reached for his sword, and then realized how useless that would be. "That snare shouldnae have struck me thus. 'Twas altered and rigged with those blooms."

She went still. "The watcher."

"I reckon 'twas him, aye," he whispered. He would have waited to see if the damage would heal, but the darkness seemed to be growing blacker. He closed his eyes and felt something hot slide down his cheek. "You must fetch help." Though his mouth formed the words, *leave me, my lady*, no sound came out. His voice had gone.

All the strength left him, and Broden toppled over as his blindness devoured him.

FROM THE TOP of the birches Cul watched

Mariena with the injured man. Backlash from the trap had badly gashed her shoulder, which still bled, but she seemed not to notice. The trapper appeared to be in far worse shape. While the swelling blisters would vanish in time, the damage done by the spell he'd added to the caustic flowers ensured this Mag Raith would never see again. The only possible cure lay in the mortal female's powerful hands.

Would she be courageous enough to use them? Cul could hardly wait to find out.

"Broden?" Mariena caught the trapper as he fell over, holding him against her body. She took hold of his face between her hands and lifted his slack head. Tears of blood streaked from his eyes to stain her fingers. "*Mon charmant*, wake up, please."

On her own face Cul saw blisters popping up, only to slowly begin shrinking. She was already absorbing his surface wounds, but she had yet to touch his eyes.

"No, no," she was muttering as she patted his cheek and shook him gently. "You must wake, for I cannot carry you myself. I will not leave you alone."

Cul sniffed the air and grimaced at the tender

scent being released by the female. These two had become lovers quite recently, but also shared an older connection. Did his former masters do nothing but allow their cullings to couple these days?

"Listen if you can hear me, Broden," Mariena said, her voice taking on a strange note. "It is not so bad. We endured much worse in the underworld, no? I am sure of it now."

She gently eased his head to the ground and took her hands away. She pressed them against her breast, staring down at him. She then reached inside her bodice, taking hold of something and wrenching out a piece of bloodied wood. She stared at it before she dropped it, and regarded the trapper.

"I must," she muttered.

Seeing her reach over and press her fingers against the trapper's eyes made Cul hold his breath.

For a time, nothing happened. It was not unexpected. The magic he'd used to blind the man was Sluath, not Pritani. It had sunk inside Broden's eyes, into the workings of the brain that allowed him to see, and distorted that into permanent darkness. Iolar had first maimed Cul with a very similar spell that had warped his bones and flesh. He could still hear his half-brother laughing as he watched the disfigurement take effect.

Cul's father, the king of the Sluath, had come to his cell later with his perfect son to survey the damage. *Why do you torment my slave-begot? His skills have proven very useful to me. Look at all the fertile slaves he's resurrected. Soon I will have a harem devoted to our bloodline.*

He is an abomination, Sire, Iolar had said. *But don't worry. His resurrection power still works, and now he can't run away.*

Mariena made a sound like a sob, blinking several times before taking her hands from the trapper's face. For a moment she wept, her shoulders shaking with the force of her sorrow, but then she lifted her face and knuckled away dark tears.

"Ne pleure pas," she said, as if speaking to someone who wasn't there. Her shoulders squared. *"Je suis le cygne."*

To Cul's astonishment she took hold of Broden under the arms and began jerking him along the trail toward the stronghold. She was trying to drag him back to the clan.

He couldn't tell if she had healed him yet or not. Climbing down from his blind seemed a terrible risk to take, especially in the daylight, but he had to know. If she still could see, then he would kill her. When he landed on the ground Mariena stopped and stared directly at him.

"Who is there?" she called out. "Edane? Nellie?"

Cul advanced on her, keeping his steps silent, and watched her face. Her gaze didn't shift, nor did her awareness of him even when he stood within arm's length. She didn't see him at all. He picked up a pebble and tossed it into the brush at his left.

Scarlet tears trickled down Mariena's cheeks as she turned toward the sound the pebble had made. The bodice of her gown slipped away from her wound. "Please, if someone is there, help me. Broden is hurt."

No, Cul thought, grinning. *He isn't.*

When his gaze shifted to her shoulder, however, his smirk faded. He didn't have to see the rest of the tattoo to know who had marked her, or why.

❧

HOT, wet drops pattering on Broden's face awoke

him, but the pain that had set his eyes and head ablaze had gone. Tugging at his shoulders and the pulling of the ground against him made it clear that someone was dragging him. Blinded now, it would be no use opening his eyes, and yet when he did they flooded with light and color.

Above him a blurred pale oval appeared, sharpening into Mariena's streaked face. She had her teeth gritted as she yanked at him, pulling him out of the forest's edge and fully into the sun. While she stared down into his face, Broden's vision sharpened. A terrible redness had turned her eyes the colors of thistles and poppies. The wetness he felt on his face was from her tears of blood.

He tried to speak to her, but his throat only produced a barely perceptible scratching sound. He'd howled himself hoarse.

"We are nearly there, I think, *mon ange*," Mariena gasped as she stopped and lifted her head as if listening. "Yes, I can hear Kiaran hammering in the forge. He hurt his back, but I could not help him. The chieftain was there."

Broden didn't understand what she meant. How could she aid the falconer? Why would it matter if Domnall saw her?

On and on she jerked him over the ground, panting through her mouth until she halted and tilted her head. "I hear them." In a much louder voice she shouted, *"Help us."*

She kept shouting it over and over, and Broden heard heavy footsteps swiftly approaching them. He turned his head to see Mael and Kiaran appear on either side of Mariena, who released his shoulders and dropped to the ground.

"Brother," the falconer said as he bent over Broden and took off his tartan to drape it over his bare chest. "'Twould seem you've outdone me this day."

"By the Gods, my lady, you bleed." Mael crouched down beside her and supported her with one big arm. "What happened?"

Broden looked past Kiaran, and saw how she flinched when the seneschal touched her. She immediately closed her eyes and averted her face. She didn't want Mael to see her, and he was convinced with the blood in her eyes she couldn't see him at all. No, it was worse than that.

Mariena had gone blind.

"Someone sabotaged one of Broden's snares," she told the men, propping her forehead against the arms she'd braced on her knees. "It struck him in the face and knocked him out. You must carry him into the stronghold for me, please. I would, but I do not think I can take another step."

Why was she trying to hide her blindness from them? Broden grabbed Kiaran's shoulder as he pushed off the tartan, hauled himself off the ground and went to her. For the moment speaking remained impossible for him, so he caught her against him and held her, stroking her disheveled hair as he tried to comfort her.

"'Twas the work of the watcher?" Mael asked, his face darkening.

Broden nodded, and then looked at Kiaran and made a slash with his fingertips across the front of his neck.

The falconer recognized the old signal they'd used as boys. "He cannot speak now. He must have shouted for help until his voice was gone." To Broden he said, "Permit Mael to carry your lady to the stronghold?"

"That won't be necessary," Mariena said. She rubbed a hand over her face before she drew back from Broden. "I am well enough to walk. Just don't ask me to carry anything."

Clear, lovely blue and gold eyes looked into Broden's, who stared back in disbelief. He had not imagined her blindness. He could still see the tracks of her scarlet tears wet on her cheeks. She smiled briefly, and then looked away.

The seneschal offered her his arm. "May I escort you, my lady?"

Kiaran picked up his tartan and looked at Broden. "So, no great harm done, then, Brother."

Broden stared after Mariena and Mael as they made their way along the trail to the stronghold. She had regained her sight almost as quickly as he had, but how? She was mortal. He wanted to snatch her back into his arms and demand to know what had happened after he'd fallen unconscious, but that would have to wait until his voice returned.

Grimly he nodded to Kiaran, and accompanied the falconer to the castle.

Once they came inside the stronghold Rosealise took one look at them and called for Edane, who hurried into the kitchens. Mariena seemed completely at ease as the shaman looked all over her face and eased the gown away from her wounded shoulder.

"This doesnae look grievous, my lady," Edane told her. "It has damaged your skinwork a little, but 'twill heal."

She glanced down at the gash that had bisected the tattoos and her face paled a little more. "So it would seem."

By then Domnall, Jenna and Nellie had joined them, and Mael related how they had found the Frenchwoman calling for help as she dragged Broden out of the forest.

"Whatever magic was used to tamper with the snare, it took away your trapper's sight for a few moments," Mariena told the chieftain after explaining what had happened. "His face also blistered for a time before he healed."

"Then 'twould seem our immortality yet heals us." Domnall sounded relieved. "What of the blood on your face, my lady?"

"She doesnae have a head wound," Edane said, frowning.

"There is blood all over us. Perhaps I touched my face after I pulled the wood from my shoulder." She showed him her stained fingers. "Other than this cut, I am fine now."

Broden stiffened. She had been blind. In that he had not been mistaken. Yet how she spoke betrayed that which he had missed.

Now Mariena was fine, just as she had been after they'd brought her to Dun Chaill. Yet after the battle with the demons her belly had been bleeding when they'd pulled her away from Edane's lady. Broden had seen the blood with his own eyes. When Nellie had awakened with no wounds they had attributed that to her attaining immortality, and the blood on Mariena from falling atop the American.

More memories came back to him. The gash on his neck had vanished the morning he'd caught her falling from the window. She'd touched his throat and quickly turned away. Just as his dislocated knee had stopped hurting a few moments after she'd put her hand over it, and then had dropped down onto the bed. He'd awakened from darkness with his sight restored to see Mariena blinded with blood in her eyes. And *now* she was fine again.

He hurt his back, but I could not help him. The chieftain was there.

It finally made sense to him. Somehow the lady was able to take the wounds from others, a power that inflicted them on her own body. She was also able to heal after the transference, almost as quickly as an immortal, but she didn't want any of them to know about her power.

Cold sweat broke out on Broden's brow. Every

power the clan possessed had limits, such as Jenna's body overheating when she passed through stone, and Domnall's difficulty in stopping himself when he moved too quickly for too long a time. Mariena had restored his vision, but what if she hadn't healed from the blinding herself? She might have spent the rest of her life in darkness.

At that moment the lady met his gaze, her lovely eyes taking on a decided shimmer before she looked away.

Chapter Eighteen

"I CANNOT BELIEVE you lost a mortal baby," Seabhag told Galan as they trudged through the overgrowth. "What did it do, crawl away while you napped under a tree?"

"I didnae sleep, and 'twas no' an infant," Galan said as he stopped and scanned a tangle of brush for any sign of movement. "Druman's an ancient druid reincarnated. He's all the memories and magics of many lifetimes, within the body of a small lad."

"Oh, so he *toddled* away from you." The demon clambered over a tangle of weeds, and shifted into the form of a mortal maiden with enormous breasts. "Druman," he called in a more feminine voice. "Come here, little one. The bad druid has gone away."

Despite the Sluath's best efforts and another hour of searching they turned up nothing.

"He's covered his tracks, but his body isnae strong enough for him to go far on foot," Galan said, forcing himself to think not as a demon but a druid. His gaze fell on an old carved ritual stone left by the remains of the tribe's blessings altar, and it came to him. "The grove."

Seabhag's breasts bounced as he trotted after him. "You think he's taken to the trees?"

"No." Galan stopped just short of the round clearing in the center of the ancient oak grove, and saw where the grass had been yanked away from stones barely protruding from the ground. When he took a step nearer he felt druid magic burning against his flesh and hastily retreated from it. "I thought he came here, but there's no sign of him."

He'd never considered that Druman had enough power to reopen a sacred grove portal, something he would have known and guarded against when he'd been a druid. The cost of his transformation by the Sluath was mounting, and made him want to kill something.

Galan forced his rage back to consider what the archivist might have done. Druman would have taken the portal back to the one nearest to the Emerald Glen tribe's settlement. Once there he would relate where Galan had taken him, and what he had done. The druids would not mistake his actions as those of Bhaltair Flen. Within a few hours the conclave would send their finest trackers out after him.

The obnoxious bairn had prevailed over him for now, but as soon as he had attained immortality he would find Druman again, and butcher him slowly.

"Bad luck, old man." Now in the form of a male wearing a strange suit and a glass circle over one eye, Seabhag clapped him on the shoulder. "We're running very low on mortals these days."

"Say what you mean," Galan muttered, slipping his hand around the iron dagger he'd concealed inside his robes.

"I mean that if you don't come back with something useful, the prince will almost certainly use you for his nightly entertainment." The demon's gloved hand reshaped into gleaming claws that strummed against Galan's neck. "I wonder if he'll let me watch you be driven insane. For you it shouldn't be much of a leap."

Galan's gaze shifted toward where he had

found Fiana's grave. Taking her bones back to Iolar and learning the prince had lied about his ability to resurrect her had nearly pushed him over the edge.

"You'll ken far more amusement when we return to the underworld," he told the Sluath.

Jerking out of Seabhag's grip, he walked away from the grove, unsure of what next to do. Since a hill sheltered the spot from the east, he changed direction and decided to climb it to look out on the lands in that direction. If the archivist had been telling the truth about the area where the hunters and their tribe had disappeared, then he could ride in that direction and see what he could find. There had to be something he could use to find Culvar before he was obliged to rejoin the demons.

The faintest shimmer of magic caught Galan's eye, and he walked toward it, expecting the unpleasant burn to increase until he had to stop. Yet as he drew closer he sensed the hovering spell to be the work of a Pritani, not druid kind.

Mayhap I dinnae have to return at all.

Drawing on his power, Galan closed his eyes and filled his senses before looking out again. Half a league away he saw a wall of enchantment stretching out in both directions, and climbing so high it seemed to disappear into the very clouds. The barrier curved slightly, engulfing the empty pastures near Wachvale as well as the deep forests that bordered it. Only a Pritani with enormous power could erect such a barrier. Edane mag Raith certainly hadn't bespelled this marvel.

"What are you doing up there?" Seabhag called from behind him. "Looking for storms? Hoping to fly away? There is no place we cannot find you, idiot."

Galan silently summoned his mortal spies to come to him before he turned and walked down the slope. He concealed his elation as he calculated how to get rid of the demon.

"We must cover more ground. Druman may have followed my horse's tracks back to the settlement. Even you should be able to do that, Seabhag." He nodded in the opposite direction. "I shall take my spies and look for him that way."

"If I don't find him, I'll keep going until I reach our little village." The demon's face contorted into that of a smirking Iolar. "Our prince does grow impatient so easily these days when he's kept waiting. I'll inform him that you've failed."

"I havenae as yet," Galan said. "How shall he react when I return with the lad, and he learns you lied to him?"

The demon's royal smirk faltered. "Pray I do not first find the brat, or all you shall have to take back to our prince will be dead meat."

Once Seabhag stalked off Galan led his small army of mortals into the woods, but then doubled back with them toward the barrier. He discovered it extended into the forest. Taking hold of the weakest mortal, Galan marched him up to the barrier and shoved him through it. The spell buckled briefly around the human, who emerged unscathed as the enchantment reformed where he had passed. For a moment his body seemed to fade, but as Galan blinked the illusion ended.

"Go after him," he said to the others.

One by one they passed unharmed through the barrier. Each time it gave way only to restore itself. All of the spies seemed unaffected by the magic.

Standing alone on the other side, Galan felt a twinge of uneasiness. Had the barrier been erected by the halfling, then it might be bespelled to kill demons. Iolar's power had altered him physically, but he remained mortal—barely, as the prince had assured him. Still, the next steps he took could lead him straight into oblivion.

He thought of Fiana as she had been after birthing Ruadri. Pale and still, her beauty forever snuffed out, she had been smiling. The midwife had claimed Fiana was glad to spend her last moments of life bringing Ruadri into the world. Galan had never questioned it—until now. He glared at the barrier as though it taunted him.

Was he to believe that Fiana had been happy, after spending hours in agonizing pain? Delighted, when she must have felt her heart slowing, and her flesh growing cold? Joyous, when she knew she would be leaving him to an eternity of loneliness without her?

His hands knotted into fists at his sides.

Why had my beloved been smiling?

Mayhap she had been trying to punish or escape him. Or she'd been so heartless as to take joy in knowing the horror and agony he would suffer. Or Fiana had never loved him at all.

"No," Galan muttered and strode into the barrier.

The magic bulged around him, hindering his steps for a brief moment before he came through on the other side. He turned around and watched a strange streak of dark blue light blaze up toward the sky before the enchantment returned to a near-invisible shimmer.

His mortal spies watched him, their faces blank and their eyes hardly blinking.

"She loved me," Galan declared as he seized the weakest by the throat, lifting him off his feet and shaking him as he would have Ruadri at birth. "Do you hear? She loved me as I loved her."

The mortal's head flopped oddly, and when Galan released him he fell to the ground dead. Echoes of what he had shouted still spread through the trees. He picked up the body and threw it through the barrier.

"Follow me, or join him," he told the rest of his spies as he turned toward the east and began to walk.

Chapter Nineteen

AS EDANE CLEANED and bandaged her shoulder Mariena felt Broden watching her. A few quick glances told her that he was probably confused, and definitely frustrated. She took care to be guarded with her words, making the sabotage sound like an accident. Of her healing she said nothing at all. Broden had been unconscious during her own bout of blindness, and she felt certain that the other men suspected nothing.

As she spoke Mariena noticed Rosealise moving abruptly away from her. She then saw Domnall make a subtle hand signal, and Mael and Kiaran left.

"'Tis fortunate Broden had you there," the chieftain said after she finished relating the incident. "With his voice gone he couldnae call for help, and we wouldnae miss him until nightfall."

Fortunate. Mariena thought of the consequences none of them knew. What had been taken from her could not have been prevented. The damage to her shoulder had caused more than pain.

Still, she'd escaped worse. Absorbing Broden's injury had been as crazy as trying to drag him back to the castle after going blind herself. She should be thanking some higher power that her vision had not been permanently destroyed. Healing the man had been an act of supreme idiocy, and yet nothing could have stopped her, not even her own fanatical sense of self-preservation.

Why did I heal him?

Her heart and her head bickered incessantly over the answer: *I had to save him.* This, for a man she'd had sex with once. She hardly knew anything about him. *My heart knows Broden.* She had not been sent here for this. She had a mission she didn't know and a power she couldn't reveal. *I should trust in him.* Now that she knew how it would end, her life would become as sand in an hourglass. *None of that matters—*

Mariena's heart declared victory as she completed the last argument.

None of that matters because I am in love with Broden.

"There, my lady." Edane frowned down at her ruined gown. "You shall wish to wash before you change your garment, but if you would, keep the bandaging dry today." To Broden he said, "One of the potions I made for Rosealise during her sickness may ease your throat, too, Brother."

"The soother, yes," the housekeeper said. "I still have a bottle of it in my chamber."

"Go with her," Domnall said to Broden.

When the chieftain saw the anger darkening the trapper's face he made the same hand signal he'd given Mael and Kiaran. The trapper gave the chieftain a hard look before he nodded and followed Rosealise out of the kitchens.

"If you're well enough, Mistress Douet," Domnall said as he turned to her, "I'd see where this mishap occurred."

Glancing down at herself, Mariena saw she had blood and dirt from their ordeal all over her. As wretched as she felt, she would have liked to spend the rest of the day scrubbing and soaking in the clan's bathing chamber. She suspected the chieftain had other reasons for leaving the stronghold with her.

As soon as they walked outside Domnall handed her a dagger and drew his own sword.

"'Tisnae like Broden to spring his own trap," he said once they had passed the gardens and entered the forest. "Some creature damaged it wriggling free. Saw you any tracks near the snare?"

"No, Chieftain." That Domnall didn't feel free to speak openly away from the castle troubled Mariena.

She led him to the berry thicket, finding the bloodstains and drag marks she'd left in the soil. All that remained of the rabbit snare lay beside the bloodied piece of wood.

"There was a white-flowered plant snarled in the trap. I think the sap from that is what blistered Broden's face." She lifted a swath of the berry shrubs to look beneath them, but didn't find a single petal.

"Mayhap the wind blew it away," Domnall suggested.

"Yes, that must be it," she replied.

Mariena straightened and carefully scanned the entire area around them. She saw no new tracks or signs that anyone had come here before them. Then she remembered the strange moment as she'd first begun dragging Broden back to the castle. She hadn't been able to see anything, but she'd felt someone close by, watching them.

The watcher knew Broden was unconscious, and I was blind. Mariena felt her palms sting but ignored it. *Then he returned to remove all traces of his tampering from the snare.*

"Thanks to you, my lady, Broden shall recover," Domnall said gently, touching her arm. "We shall take measures to assure 'twillnae happen again."

She loosened her white-knuckled hands before her fingernails broke the skin. "That would be wise."

Walking back to the stronghold Mariena looked at everything they passed for signs of the watcher. Their silent enemy had disturbed nothing in the forest. She didn't spot a single track that didn't belong to her, Domnall and Broden. Then she noticed something odd about Broden's boot prints, which looked deeper than the chieftain's despite the fact that Domnall was larger and heavier than his trapper.

The watcher uses our tracks to cover his own.

She eyed the deeper tracks, which veered off from the trail toward the barn, then grew lighter again just beside the curtain wall. Jenna had told her the castle had bespelled arches that appeared to lead the unwary into rooms filled with magic traps. The watcher would know where they were and how to use them to move through the castle. He'd probably set the traps not to be triggered by his presence.

"Chieftain, this scroll that Rosealise found in her chamber, might I borrow it?" she asked as they walked back along the trail. "I do not know the castle very well yet. The map would help me to better find my way until I become more familiar with the place, no? And I should like to do that now, if I may."

Understanding glinted in the chieftain's eyes. "Aye, 'twould be helpful to you. 'Tis kept in the forge."

Chapter Twenty

THE FOREST AHEAD proved dense and seemed endless to Galan, who looked for but saw no signs of anyone occupying or working the place. He continued on until the sun dipped down to the horizon, and the trees began to thin. The sound of rushing water drew him toward the border of a clearing, where he looked out at a winding, sparkling river. An oddly blank and sunken patch of earth caught his eye.

As he approached and crouched next to the shallow hole, he noted the barrel-sized boulders that bordered it. Judging from the depth of the depression and the still damp soil at its bottom, he reckoned that another boulder had once occupied the spot. He stood and surveyed the vicinity, finally spotting a boulder on the other bank that not only corresponded in size, but bore the dark stain of dirt on one side.

The hair prickled on the back of his neck. No force of nature had levitated the large stone and deposited it on the other side of the water. Someone had thrown it there. Galan knew of only one man with that kind of strength: Broden mag Raith.

Had the halfling and the hunters joined forces? That would be an unlikely but very interesting development. Culvar had gone to great lengths to trap the Sluath in the mortal realm while concealing his existence from the demons. Like him, the Mag Raith had escaped the underworld, and shared his hatred for Iolar and his brethren. Such an alliance might prove quite lethal for the demons.

Galan smiled, imagining the prince's reaction to learning that his grotesque half-brother still lived, just in time to be murdered by him and the hunters.

Studying the forest on the other side of the water, Galan spotted even more intriguing details. Above the very tops of the trees the jagged silhouette of a stone tower rose. Peering carefully, he made out another with a weathered, splintered peak roof, and patches of ashlar closer to the ground. From the expanse of it he felt certain the stone had once formed a curtain wall.

"Hide yourselves, keep your daggers ready, and await my command," he told his spies, who silently scattered.

Galan made his way down to where he could use brush and stones as cover while he crossed the river. On the other side he darted into the trees, and listened for sounds of anyone approaching before he moved deeper into the forest. He took his time to assure he would not be discovered, and soon came to the edge of the woods. Across a clearing stood the ruins of an immense castle, likely abandoned for centuries. Yet as he studied the front of the stronghold he saw where the walls had been repaired, and a new roof atop one of the many towers. A pair of small raptors perched on the battlements, their black eyes searching the grounds below them. Galan recognized both from the many centuries they had done the same for their master in the Moss Dapple's forest.

Kiaran mag Raith's kestrels guarded the castle.

Slipping back behind a wide trunk, Galan

altered the spell of his body ward, covering himself with green, brown and glowing patches. The camouflage concealed him as he made a slow circuit of the walls, and noted all the work that had been done to repair its defenses. The hunters must have dwelled here since they'd left the Moss Dapple's enchanted forest.

By the time he reached the river again Galan hadn't seen any of the hunters or their females, but that didn't concern him. Finding a way into the stronghold while remaining undetected did. As he moved into the gardens in the back of the ruins he considered waiting until nightfall, and then saw a swatch of shadows emerge from the forest to go to a barn, and there step out into the sunlight.

The cloaked being moved across the open ground quickly, yet with a lurching movement that made Galan think of a horse that had gone lame. It entered an arch that formed in the curtain wall, and then vanished. Galan sniffed the air until he caught the shadowy creature's scent, which smelled of two very different things: ancient Pritani magic and immortal demonic flesh.

Culvar.

Having found his quarry would have gratified

Galan, but the halfling's stink made his gut clench and his heart pound in a different fashion. A peculiar bloodlust rose inside him, chilling and ravenous. He wanted to chase after Culvar, but not to capture him and force him to do his bidding. No, all he desired was to chain the outcast to a tree and skin him slowly while he listened to him beg for mercy.

If the slightest whiff of the halfling could make Galan feel so brutal, then it must have driven Prince Iolar to madness.

He heard a distant commotion and several voices. Retreating deeper into the forest, he commanded his spies to climb the trees and better conceal themselves among the branches. Using the available cover, he went in the direction of the sounds. There he watched as an unfamiliar, battered-looking mortal female and Domnall mag Raith emerge from the stronghold. After arming the mortal, the chieftain drew his sword and led her along the same trail into the forest that Culvar had used to leave it.

Perhaps you have not formed an alliance after all.

Galan's thirst for blood grew almost unbearable as he watched the arrogant Pritani disappear into the trees. How he would love nothing more than to chase down Domnall and use his power to torment and then obliterate the smug bastart. Bitterly he clamped down on his raging hunger for vengeance. While he felt certain with Iolar's power infusing him he could prevail over a single Mag Raith, he could not take on the other four by himself...unless he could attack them one at a time.

He eyed the curtain wall where Culvar had disappeared, and muttered a spell under his breath. The stone sparkled with Pritani magic, exactly as had the sealed gates to the underworld. To try and breach it while still mortal would likely kill him, Galan thought, feeling frustrated now. With the sun climbing high in the sky he couldn't risk entering the stronghold where he might be caught by the clan. One partially rebuilt tower tempted him, for it appeared empty, and would likely provide access to passages within the keepe. He suspected once inside he could find a place to conceal himself until nightfall.

Kiaran mag Raith came out of the barn near Galan, forcing him to go still. At the falconer's side walked Nellie Quinn, the touch-reader who had been killed during their battle with the demons. He'd watched her die as he'd escaped with Iolar. Now she appeared not only alive, but radiant with a unique glow that only one thing gave to a human.

They resurrected the deceitful slut, and gave her the gift of eternal life.

To see such a conniving whore enjoying the gift ever denied his beloved Fiana made Galan shake with fury. Yet when Kiaran halted, he still had enough control to shadow his body ward so that he might blend in with the forest.

The falconer's shoulders twitched as he stared directly at Galan, and for a moment he thought his ruse had not worked. Then Kiaran murmured something to Nellie, who nodded and walked with him into the castle.

Galan remained where he was, watching as Domnall and the pale-haired mortal returned to the castle. Once they had disappeared inside, he trotted quickly to the ruined tower, and stepped through the gap in the stones.

Chapter Twenty-One

AFTER FETCHING THE potion from Rosealise's chamber, Broden remained with the housekeeper in the kitchens, where he paced. Domnall had signaled all the men to guard their ladies, which made his mood even more foul. He wanted to take Mariena somewhere he could speak with her alone, and discover her reason for concealing her power. Why had she taken his blindness from him? Did she know their powers had limits? How could she have been so rash? To have his vision restored at the cost of Mariena's own sight would have ended him.

A trill of cold laughter echoed in his skull. *Yer selfishness made ye immortal. Ye'd survive.*

"Come now, my dear sir," Rosealise said as

she filled a mug with a fragrant brew. "You should have this lavender chamomile tisane with Edane's potion. The hot drink shall help the medicine work."

Although the roughness in his throat had already eased, to please her Broden drank down the honeyed herbal concoction and then sipped her flowery brew. The attack had stirred his power, now temper-strained and eager to be released, and he needed a more physical distraction. He went to the wood pile and began snapping arm-thick splits into fist-size chunks for the cooking hearth, hoping that would appease it.

"Broden, please." Rosealise came and offered him a smooth wooden pegged handle. "If you must pit your strength against something, let it be a heap of grain."

"Aye." The word came out as if the quern had lodged itself in his throat, but at least he could make some sound. He walked over to her work table and fitted the handle in the large circular handstone before pouring some oats into the center hollow, which emptied onto the saddle stone beneath it.

The housekeeper came over with a clean

empty sack, which she put to one side. "I know gentlemen in this time regard such work as a lady's domain, but I confess, we hate grinding grain, probably more than you do. It requires such effort for very scant results."

Broden glanced at the slow sift of the powdery oat flour and nodded. Even with his strength he'd barely ground a handful.

"Which reminds me," Rosealise said, "your lady had a smashing idea."

The housekeeper related Mariena's suggestion for creating a water-powered millhouse. With his strength and Jenna's aid, they could see it done.

"I do not wish to add to your worries," Rosealise said in a low voice, "but while we have this moment alone I'd like to confide something, if I may." She sighed. "Lately I've noticed an oddity about my persuasion power. Since the night of the battle with the Sluath it has been almost, ah, directing me to use it."

He frowned at her, unsure of her meaning.

"When someone speaks untruthfully now, I feel a distinct urge to touch them," she said. "Such as when my dearest husband claimed my chicken and leek stew was top-notch. I simply could not keep my hand from him, which is how I learned that he's never cared for leeks. Mael admitted that he lied to spare my feelings."

Broden wondered why the housekeeper was telling him this, and then recalled how earlier she had quickly retreated across the kitchens. "Mariena."

"Yes. When she spoke of your accident, I again felt the urge. It came with such insistence that I had to move away from her." Rosealise's expression grew pained. "I cannot but wonder why I am now gripped with such a need. The only circumstance that has changed here at Dun Chaill has been Mariena's arrival."

Mael walked in with Jenna from the keepe, and then Kiaran arrived with Nellie from the dairy barn. While the housekeeper went to relate to the women what had happened, the two men took up positions by the entries to keep watch. Edane returned with daggers and sheaths that he wordlessly gave to the ladies. Even Rosealise, who hated weapons, reluctantly tied the sheathed blade to her waist sash.

When the shaman came over to the quern Broden eyed him. "I speak again."

"Dinnae yet," Edane said, peering at him for a moment. In a lower voice he said, "'Twasnae an injury that took your sight. I see spelltrace in your eyes, Brother."

Broden felt fear swell inside him. Mariena had not only taken his blindness, she had absorbed the watcher's magic. Magic that the fiend had used to kill countless mortals. With his powers he could have altered the spell to have a different effect on her. The watcher had already hurled Rosealise back to the underworld, and nearly buried Nellie alive.

Mariena might have died to save his comely, worthless hide.

Dimly he heard a cracking sound, and the handstone suddenly shattered in three pieces. Rosealise gasped as Broden stepped back from the stand, which made a creaking sound before the broken quern dropped through the frame and smashed on the floor.

He stared at it and his dust-covered hands.

The housekeeper came to survey the rubble. "Well, you've done me a great service, my dear sir," she said briskly. "I absolutely despised that wretched thing."

Broden heard compassion as well as truth in her voice, but it didn't change what he had done. If he lost control of his power, he'd be as much a danger to the clan as the watcher.

"Forgive me." He strode out of the kitchens.

❧

ONCE THEY HAD RETRIEVED the scroll from the forge, Domnall escorted Mariena to her chamber so she could wash and change. He offered to wait outside in the passage for her, but she knew he wanted to return to see that the women were safe and his men on their guard.

"I will be fine, Monsieur," she assured him, and saw Broden at the other end of the passage going into his chamber. Back at the forge she had promised to take one of the men with her while she searched for the watcher. "I will ask your trapper to accompany me while I explore the castle today. He can keep me out of trouble, no?"

"Aye." The chieftain handed her the weapons and sheaths he'd taken from Kiaran's work bench, all glittering and honed with lethal-fine edges. "I'll speak with you later, my lady."

Inside her room Mariena stripped out of her

filthy gown and scrubbed herself, growing grim as she cleaned the blood from her face and hands and hair. Braiding her wet mane back, she changed into the trousers and tunic Jenna had given her, and strapped the sheathed sword to her waist. Drawing it, she adjusted her belt to ride lower on her hips, and then tucked the two sheathed daggers inside her garments.

The cool weight of the weapons made her feeling of vulnerability vanish, as if they were clothes and she had been walking about naked for days.

Unrolling the scroll map on her table, Mariena studied the intricate drawing of the castle. While they'd been inside the forge Domnall had showed her the symbols indicating the different traps and explained how they had secured most by blocking them off. She doubted the watcher would hide inside a trap room, but the arrangement of the different deadly caches suggested to her that he might be using them to enter concealed passages connected to them.

Once decided on the route she would take, Mariena placed the scroll back in its sleeve and tucked it under her belt. She would search every inch of this castle until she found the watcher, but she would not capture or deliver him to the Mag Raith. For what the watcher had done to Broden, she would kill him. Finally she didn't care about the blackness in her heart.

She left her room and walked down the passage to Broden's door, stopping there as she considered breaking her promise to Domnall. She knew only too well the hell the trapper had suffered, believing himself blinded. She also didn't want him to stop her from gutting the watcher.

Then again, he might wish to help her with that.

The door swung open, and Broden looked out at her with his clear, beautiful dark eyes. Like her he had changed and washed, and his wet hair hung around his flawless features in enticing disarray. He regarded her without smiling, and yet she sensed something had altered his mood. Last night he had been determined to be rid of her, and now he appeared as if he wanted to drag her inside and never let her out again.

No, she thought. *That is what you want him to do.*

"You don't have to speak, *mon charmant,*" Mariena assured him, folding her arms to keep herself from running her fingers through his sleek mane. "It is only that I am exploring the castle, and your chieftain does not wish me to wander alone." She made the hand signal that Domnall had taught her, one that meant she hunted dangerous prey. "Would you accompany me?"

For a moment his expression grew fierce, as if he meant to do as she had imagined. Then he turned, retrieved his sword, and stepped out to join her.

"The chamber where Rosealise first stayed is just around the corner, no?" she asked, although she knew the answer as she walked in that direction. "She said to me she left a gown there that I might use. Since I am ruining everything I wear, I think I should."

Mariena continued the harmless chatter as they approached the chamber, and tucked a hand around her sword hilt as Broden took down a torch and unlatched the door. She slipped inside, breathing in deeply but smelling only dampness and the ashes in the cold hearth.

Beneath the musty scents, however, lurked something menacing.

Broden stayed close to her as she moved inside. Mariena knew from what Domnall had told her that the arch that had led Mael and Rosealise to become trapped in the vine room lay on the other side of the bed. The scroll map had been planted in the same spot as a lure, so the watcher had been obliged to access the chamber himself. She turned slowly, inspecting the walls for any sign of another entrance, but saw none.

"I think Rosealise did not belong in such a small space," Mariena said as she went around the bed and crouched down to look at the cracks in the mortar where the arch had opened. They extended on either side, but not across the floor. "A woman of her stature would need more room—and how sturdy is this bed?"

She shoved it away from the cracks in the wall, but saw no sign of any seams in the floor beneath it. Her shoulder began to throb as she straightened and examined the walls again. Then a fragment of grass drifted down in front of her nose, and she tipped her head back. The thatching above the bed looked well-woven into the twisted branches supporting it, but some of the bundles appeared newer than the others.

A strong hand caught her arm, startling her. "My lady."

Broden's voice had returned, as rough as before, but softer now as well. The combination made him sound as he had when they'd made love. A bloom of pain and the direction of his gaze made her reach for her shoulder, and she felt a large wet patch where her wound had bled through her tunic.

Naturally she could heal anyone but herself, Mariena thought impatiently. "It's nothing." She met his gaze. "I will change the bandage later."

He shook his head and gripped her arm. "Now." He steered her toward the door.

She walked back with him, but instead of going to her chamber he took her to his. Once inside he pointed to his bed and took a satchel from under his bench.

"I can attend to it myself," Mariena told him. "I only need some clean linen."

Broden came and motioned for her to take off her tunic as he removed a bundle of cloth and a jar from the satchel. Once she pulled off the tunic all that covered her was the thin chemise under it, but when she tugged it down he seemed interested only in her wound.

"You don't have to—ah." She hissed in a breath as he pressed a cloth to the bleeding gash and applied painful pressure. "I'm not helpless, *mon ami*, and I know you want no more to do with me."

Mariena hated how hurt she sounded, but that came from a very different ache. Yet when she looked into his eyes again she saw anguish there, too.

"I told you that I dreamed of you," Broden said, speaking only a little above a whisper now. "Weeks before the battle you came to me, every night. In my dreams we didnae battle in an arena. We shared a bed, and more pleasures than I've ever ken. We spoke of love as mates long bonded and never to part."

In that moment she would have given anything to have all her memories restored. "Why did you keep this from me?"

"When you came to Dun Chaill, you didnae recognize me. You held my dagger to my throat." Broden lifted the cloth to inspect the gash. "The vision we shared last night, that, too, made me reckon my dreams unreal. That I'd taken and shaped a memory of you to suit my own longing." He opened the jar and began gently applying a salve to her wound that smelled of herbs and honey. "'Tis been driving me mad, no' to ken the truth."

She watched him roll a clean bandage around her shoulder. Every time he touched her she felt her skin tingle, and her body ache for him. But he had taken hold of her heart, as surely as if it already belonged to him.

Maybe it had.

"We are not dreamers, *mon ange*. We are practical, you and I. Last night showed me what we could be together. I want to know what we were, too." She reached out and touched his face. "There is one way."

Broden looked at her for a long, silent moment, and then went to bar the door.

When he returned Mariena removed her weapons and held them out to him. "Put them in your trunk with your blades."

MARIENA WATCHED as Broden placed the weapons inside his trunk, which he bound with rope that he tossed over a rafter and used to heft it out of their reach. She glanced around the room before she pushed his unused firewood far out of reach under his bed. That left the torch still burning in the wall bracket, which he took down and plunged into his water pail before tossing into the hearth.

The only light in the room now came from the sun slanting through his narrow window, which shone between them like a glowing wall.

"'Tis a grievous risk, my lady," he said as they faced each other. "I cannae vow we'll share a vision, or emerge from another unscathed."

"You're immortal, *mon ami*." Mariena took a step closer as she tugged off her stained chemise. She felt surer of this, of him, than anything she'd done since coming to the castle. "And I am not so easy to kill, I think."

Broden pulled off his tunic to bare the skin-work on his arm. His hand remained steady as he reached through the light to touch her face. "'Tis madness, what we do."

She rubbed her cheek against his fingers, delighting in the glide of his hard flesh against her soft skin. "To do mad things is what bravery is, no?"

The light from the window grew brighter, gilding his dark hair and his broad shoulders. It spilled over her hands as she sifted her fingers through his sleek mane and brought his mouth to hers. Stealing a kiss before they fell into a vision of the wretched underworld felt like putting armor over their souls. Ending it felt like tearing her heart from her breast.

"We shouldnae," he muttered against her lips, his arms closing around her.

Mariena felt his body tensing against hers, and her own softened. "This is how it began the last time, no?" Boldly she slipped her hand between them, covering and stroking the hard length of his erection. "Naked in your bed, with you inside me." She felt him swell against her palm. "Ah, you remember now."

"Demons couldnae make me forget." He lifted her off her feet, walking with her to the bed. There he set her down, dragging his arms away from her. "I wager we've only to touch our ink together to share a vision."

"I prefer to be thorough." She stripped to her skin, and lay back on his bed linens. "But you can touch any part of me that you wish, *mon charmant*. Show me how I was for you in your dreams."

Broden's eyes shifted as he looked at her from her eyes to her toes, and back again. Silently he took off his boots and trousers, and then sat down beside her. "You truly wish to ken?"

"I could beg, if you like." Mariena shifted over

to make room for him. As he stretched out beside her she sensed his desire growing as thick and heavy as his straining erection. "In your dreams of me, did I say please, Broden, love me now? That I shake with wanting your body on mine, your cock inside me? For you see I do. I think you like me to beg."

"Aye, for me." He put his hand on her waist to pull her against him, and draped her thigh over his. "'Tisnae kind."

"Why would you be kind in bed?" She ran her hands over his glorious chest to feel the hard muscle under his flawless skin. "I like it when you are demanding. It is passionate. We are both passionate people."

"You're no' my bed slave," he told her roughly.

"I am not like your poor mother, *mon ange*." She saw the hurt in his eyes and kissed his mouth. "I give you this. I want your passion to take over me. It sets me free. You make me be who I dream I am. Yours."

Broden took her mouth and pulled her hips against his. The first touch of him against the pulsing seam of her sex made her go molten, and against her lips he murmured her name.

"There, yes." She couldn't think of anything

more than taking him inside her. "Make my dreams come true."

Broden rolled onto his back at the same moment he penetrated her, lifting and impaling her softness on the swollen column of his penis. He held her as she cried out, steadying her as he watched her face. "Dance on me, my lady."

Mariena sank down on him, her hands clutching his shoulders and her head falling back as the heady sensations of being so completely filled flowed through her. His heat followed the bright aching pleasure, suffusing her sex and racing up into her breasts. His hands cupped and held her mounds, squeezing her tight nipples as he arched under her, driving deeper.

"'Tis just as you came to me in the night." He grunted as she tightened around him. "Again and again you took me in your quim, and moaned for me, and steeped me in your sweet pleasures. You never denied me. 'Twas as I dreamed."

Fucking him like this was going to make her come so hard that she might hurl them both into a vision. She took hold of his inked arm, and held it down against the ticking as she worked herself on his engorging shaft. Stroking her pussy over him made her pant and swell within, so that she felt more acutely each thrust of his cock. She never wanted to stop, but when he took hold of her bottom and drove her down to his root, her body fused with her emotions.

Broden. Her thoughts spun away in a whirling tempest of joy and relief and love.

Mariena fell over on him, trembling and wild with bliss. For a time, all she could do was tremble and gasp and cling to him. She felt him still iron-hard inside her, and managed to lift her head. Broden looked as if he'd joined her in the climax, his satisfaction so evident in his eyes they glittered like dark jewels on fire.

"Now you," she begged him. "Make me your dream woman. Show me how you took me in the night."

Broden gripped her waist, lifting her off his cock and putting her on her hands and knees. He came up behind her, his fist guiding his cockhead to her slick folds before he plunged in deep, pulling her back against him at the same time. The thrust of his hips slapped against her bottom as he plowed into her pussy, his cock entrancing her to become as quivering and helpless as she burned to be for him.

"I had you thus," he told her, his breath

caressing her ear. "Mine to fack as I pleased. 'Tis what made you wild for me, for more."

If only she had eternity, Mariena thought, for him to spend himself in her. She could see losing herself in the ecstasy of yielding to his passion, and the glory of knowing only she could give him what he needed. No matter how many times they took each other, it would never be enough. They could come together every hour, every moment, and it would not satisfy either of them.

Broden filled his hands with her breasts as he pumped harder and faster into her body. "You shall come on my cock again, my lady, as I fill you with my cream. Give me all your pleasures, Mariena, now."

Tears slipped down her face as she let go of her fear and sorrow, and let the last, impossibly deep stroke of his cock ignite her. She gripped him with the rhythm of the stream of euphoria that smashed through her, and felt his cock pulse as he emptied his seed into her clasping softness.

They fell on their sides together, dazed and slick with sweat. Mariena could hardly move for the tremors that racked her, but then she felt the ink on her breast warming. He had put his marked arm around her to bring her closer, and it had come too close to her Sluath tattoo.

"Broden, wait," she begged.

The chamber blurred, and then shrank in on them as the smooth walls grew rough and began to curve.

Chapter Twenty-Two

SEEING MARIENA AND Broden entering the unused chamber that held the entrance to the vine room intrigued Cul, who had thought the healer would have taken to her bed after her busy morning. Had they attempted to access his trap, he could have quickly retreated out of sight, but they had kept back from the wall.

The healer had proven resilient, but she remained mortal. Cul suspected that compelling Mariena to heal him would likely end her life. Still, she would resurrect as an immortal. He wouldn't have believed it possible outside the underworld, and yet the other women had proven it could happen. Her immortality would make her his forever. He had never attempted to keep a human without enchantment. That would require building a chamber to keep her secure.

It does not have to be as it was for slaves in the underworld. If she accommodates me, I'll allow her to keep her pretty lover.

Unease crept up Cul's bent back as soon as Mariena strained her wounded shoulder. Only after some moments did he realize the scent of her bleeding was what disconcerted him. Alive, she smelled even more delicious than a fresh kill. The hunger, however, perplexed him. Even while enslaved in the underworld he had never fed on mortals. To him it would have been the same as gnawing on his own body. Some of the more brutal demons, however, took great pleasure in tormenting their slaves by eating their flesh.

What had stirred his long-despised Sluath half?

Once the pair left the room Cul climbed into the rafters, moving past the thatching he'd replaced as he tracked them by the blood scent to Broden's chamber. Carefully he looked down through a gap in the yelms to see Mariena remove her tunic. Their desire at once tainted the air.

Since he had no interest in watching them couple, he decided to retreat back into his underground tunnels. As Broden had uncovered the healer's bleeding wound, however, Cul froze. The gash inflicted by the blinding snare had cut completely through her Sluath ink. Without realizing it he'd ruined Mariena's tattoo—the one thing that would keep him from breaking the only promise he'd ever made.

Vow to me ye shall never again use yer Sluath power, the beautiful slave had demanded. *That ye willnae raise another mortal from the dead.*

Bitter self-disgust made bile fill Cul's mouth, and compelled him to open an old arch in the outer wall beside him. He leaned into it to puke, but lost his balance and fell. Dropping through the shaft into the passage below, he landed heavily, and felt his arm snap beneath him. Biting back a howl of agony, he jerked his broken limb out and held it as the bones knitted back together.

He lay on his back and stared up through the passage over him, his thoughts in a hopeless snarl. He could not break his vow to the strange slave who had saved his life and helped him flee to the mortal realm. That promise had done more than allow him to escape enslavement. It had been the foundation on which he had built Dun Chaill.

I never wanted my power, Cul had told the slave

after he finished laughing at her. *The king forced me to use it to provide him with breeders. So yes, I swear to you, I will never again resurrect a mortal.*

For centuries he had resisted the taint of his immortal sire's blood by using only Pritani magic, of which he'd become a master. Unlike the Sluath, Cul had killed only to protect himself, when he might have ravaged the mortal realm at his whim. He'd shown mercy to the Mag Raith and their females, even when the wiser course would have been to slaughter them all. Yet while watching the healer he'd thought of imprisoning her. He'd even hungered for her flesh. Such desires had never been his…except when he had drawn too close to his infernal half-brother.

Cul pushed himself upright.

Could Iolar have found his way to Dun Chaill? Why hadn't the barrier alerted him?

He tasted the air, drawing unsteady gulps of it over his sensitive tongue. He'd grown accustomed to the smells of his unwanted guests, but now he detected someone who did not belong to the clan. This new intruder shed both the heat of a mortal and the icy power of a Sluath prince. Then a sickly rush of emotions followed, and Cul recognized their particular stench.

Galan Aedth.

Of course Iolar had given some of his own power to his pet druid. That was what had roused Cul's Sluath senses. Galan also still remained mortal enough to pass through the barrier.

Cul hoisted himself onto his feet, clutched his crooked arm, and dragged his ruined leg as he followed the stink of the druid.

Chapter Twenty-Three

DEEP IN THE passages of the underworld, Mariena led her Pritani lover through the maze of tunnels. Soon the Sluath would leave for the mortal realm in order to cull more souls to turn into slaves. That would be their only window of opportunity, Jenna had told her, and they could only attempt this once. Mariena had to be sure exactly where to go when the time came for them and their friends to escape.

One mistake, pal, the architect had told her, *and we all die.*

Mariena's diaphanous gown swirled around her legs as she stopped at the edge of the tunnel. From that position she checked the long passage ahead of them until she spied the tiny line and circle scratched beside a gap in the stone.

"There." She pointed at it. "Jenna said the demon would mark the place. Behind that gap is where the portal will be on the night of the culling feast. We will meet with the others in the tunnels and go in there together. It will bypass the guarded areas and take us to–"

Broden jerked her back into the shadows and pressed her against the wall, covering her mouth with his hand. A few moments later a guard trudged past them, dragging the limp, battered body of a Viking behind him. Once the Sluath had gone, Broden took his hand away.

"You have ears like a cat," Mariena whispered.

"I dinnae care for yer scheme. 'Tis too much like their torments." Before she could answer he peered at the marked gap and shook his head. "Look at the opening. 'Tis too small for any but Nellie, or mayhap Edane. If the traitor wishes to expose us–"

"*Merde alors.* Everything is not a trap, *mon couer.*" Mariena leaned out to check the tunnel. "The demon promised to make it larger when the time comes for our escape. For now, it must remain like this so it goes undetected."

The trapper eyed the constricted space again. "And 'twillnae collapse when we're within?"

"Jenna promised the demon will keep it open." The sound of stone shifting in the distance made her suppress a shudder. "It is simple, Broden. We have all worked together on this plan. Domnall and Jenna trust this demon. You trust them." She smiled. "As for me, I trust no one but you. So, if it is a trap, it will be your fault."

"Dinnae jest," he muttered tightly. "I cannae go on without ye, *a thasgaidh*. If ye're taken from me, and given to another–"

"There will be no other," Mariena said, reminding him of the pact they had made. "Trust me, Broden. This is the best chance we have to leave this place. We must take it."

He took hold of her hand as they carefully made their way back through the maze of passages. Although the prospect of being found outside their cell was always a risk, it was the man beside her who caused her heart to begin pounding madly. His touch made her wish she could stop and find a niche where they might steal a moment for themselves. She wanted him now as she always did, naked and in her arms, murmuring her name. When they passed an alcove where they might hide for a moment she couldn't help tugging at his arm.

"I am trying to be a woman now," she told him. "We have time for a kiss."

"Ye ever say that, and then I cannae stop kissing ye," he told her, cradling her face and brushing his thumb over her lips.

"I know. Then you must take off my gown and put your hands on my body." Mariena pressed up against him. "And call me your bed slave as you come inside me. They will never know that you've become my bed slave."

He uttered a low laugh. "'Tis what ye've made of me with yer sweet surrendering."

"We are both enslaved now, I think." She sighed and pressed her cheek against his chest. "Only you must learn French after we leave this place. Your language is too hard for words of love."

His arms tightened around her. "If the demon lies, and we dinnae find each other once we return to the mortal realm–"

"Then I'll do as I promised," she assured him. "You cannot escape me, *mon couer*."

"That I ken, for I feel the same for ye. I shall hunt ye forever if I must." Broden pulled her against him, holding her for a long moment. "Come."

They reached the portal they had used to access the tunnels, and together stepped through the glowing arch. Instead of emerging in the chamber where they'd been kept imprisoned, Mariena saw a wide oval of white-blue sand heavily spattered with blood and gore. She recognized it as the arena where slaves were pitted against each other to fight to the death. The tiers of stone encircling it appeared empty, which confused her more until she realized what had happened.

"The demon moved the wretched portal," she muttered to Broden. "Seabhag must have come to the chamber to check on us, and found it empty."

"Aye, 'tis likely." He put his arm around her as he scanned the stands of the arena. "I dinnae see any demons here. We'll go to one of the torment chambers, and say that a guard took us."

A cloaked figure appeared behind him, two swords glittering in its claws, and Mariena's heart sank. "Too late for that, *mon couer*."

Broden glanced over his shoulder, and then

shook his head. "I cannae fight ye," he told her, his voice tight.

"You must, my Pritani," she whispered, "or we both die."

She ran from him, hoping it would look as if she were trying to get away from him. She thought of Paris, and then stopped and turned. Hatred flooded into her, fueling her ruse with all the darkness in her heart.

"You think you can put your hands on me, and I will do nothing?" Shouting at him and kicking the sand wasn't enough, however. "I'll never spread my legs for a demon."

"I told ye, I'm no' Sluath," Broden muttered. He didn't have to pretend to be angry. His eyes burned with it. "Ye're my slave now, wench. Accept your fate."

A robed figure flung two short swords into the center of the sands before stepping back into the shadows. Broden snatched up the blades, tossing one to Mariena, who caught it reflexively. She should have charged him while he was straightening, but instead she retreated, hoping the traitor could somehow get them out of this before they were discovered.

Broden looked sick, his face gleaming with sweat.

"The only thing you'll put in my belly, Pritani, is that blade," Mariena taunted as she matched his movements.

Her voice echoed in the emptiness of the arena, but the fine hairs on her arms bristled as she heard approaching footsteps. She moved until she could see the two demons who emerged from the tunnel at Broden's left. Both looked like boys, but one blurred and shimmered as his shape changed into that of a wrinkled old man.

Seabhag, who had told her what he would do if he ever found her outside Broden's prison chamber.

Have you ever seen a man whipped to death? Try and escape again, you vicious little miss, and I'll beat him until all that's left are bits of pretty flesh hanging from his bones.

Broden came running straight at her, just as they had rehearsed in the mock fights they'd practiced in his cell. He remembered to close his eyes a moment before she tossed the sand in his face, and then stumbled back as if she'd blinded him.

Mariena advanced quickly, hating herself as she struck a glancing blow at him. He turned, but not enough to avoid her blade, which slashed across his chest. Little more than a scratch, the wound she left on him still made her stomach surge.

Broden sprang at her and knocked her onto the sands. As they'd practiced in secret, she feigned rage and released the sword a moment before he kicked it away from her hand.

I love this man, Mariena thought as she got to her feet. *Nothing will keep us apart. I will kill anything that tries.*

The fear left his eyes, replaced by a love just as deep and determined as her own.

She screamed and hurled herself at him.

❧

BRODEN CAUGHT Mariena as she slammed into him, but this time he fell back with her through a blur of time. They landed not on the sands of the arena but the bed in his chamber. As before when they'd emerged from the vision they both went still and stared at each other.

"'Twasnae a real battle," he said, relishing the relief the truth had brought to him, and the delight of discovering his dreams had been memories. "By the Gods. We feigned everything so the demons would believe you ran from me."

"Trés bon." She collapsed against him, her hair spilling over his chest. "But I can run no longer. You will have to bring food and drink to me here now. I am never leaving this bed again."

He felt something wet on his neck, and felt her tremble. He wrapped his arms around her, holding her as she wept without a sound. The terrible burden of believing he'd hurt her in the arena, now gone, left but one shadow on his heart. They had loved each other in the underworld, but there had he told her of Sileas, and his death trap? Could she have fallen in love with him if he had?

"You had better stop me, or I think I will drown you," Mariena said, her damp mouth brushing over his scar. "So, I was pretending to be your bed slave, but you were mine."

"I'm yours now," he said, stroking her back. "But you maynae want me when you learn the truth."

"The truth can wait until a very long time from now." She shifted up on him. "Make love to me again, please. This makes me happy."

With her soft and willing in his arms, the scent

of their bodies and their pleasures mingling, it would have made him very happy to take her again. Yet Broden knew he had to tell her everything. "My lady, 'tis something you dinnae ken of me."

"Pah. I know you, *mon charmant.* I have kissed every inch of you, no? And you probably told me and forgot you did." Mariena pushed herself up and glared down at him. "Also, I am trying to be a woman again. Don't ruin my moment."

"I'd deny you naught, my lady, but 'tis time for truth between us." Even as he knew his confession might cost him everything, he couldn't truly be hers unless she knew. "You reckoned I'd never harm a female. You dinnae ken what I did in my mortal life. I've concealed that from everyone, even my brothers."

"Everyone has secrets." She looked all over his face, and then sighed. "Very well. Tell me this truth."

Broden lifted her away and rose from the bed. After he pulled on his trews and gathered her garments for her, he went to look out through the narrow window while she dressed. Allowing the sun to warm his face was almost as good as kissing

Mariena. He'd never cared for darkness, which had terrified him as a lad.

Yet moving toward the light was not the same as being part of it. That he understood.

Telling her proved easy at first. She already knew of his birth, so he related how he'd been taken in by the Mag Raith as a bairn, and fostered by the tribe.

"My sire came to the settlement but rarely. When he did, he spent much time with Domnall's sire, Nectan, attending to tribal matters. I'd be presented, but he said little to me, and ever looked away from my face." Broden smiled a little. "I reminded him of my *máthair*, for I didnae resemble him. And she'd been his favorite."

He told Mariena how he'd been cared for by the adults of the Mag Raith tribe, who had done only what was needed to train him to look after himself. As he grew it had been his physical beauty that had caused resentment among some of the other lads. From them he'd learned the cause of the scar on his throat, and the ruin of his voice. In time he'd also discovered his mother's enslavement and death in childbirth, and how he'd been sent away after his sire's mate had tried to strangle him. Only Kiaran, another outcast, had befriended him.

He admitted he never realized how badly tainted he was, being the son of a bed slave, until Eara had declared her love for him to his sire.

"He shamed the lass in front of the entire tribe for losing her heart to a slaveborn with naught," Broden said.

Finally, he had to tell her of the day he'd learned the truth of his status in the worst possible manner. He remembered every moment of it, etched in horror and rage as it was in his memory.

"My sire died defending my birth tribe from the Carrack tribe," Broden said. "'Twas his mate, Sileas, came to tell me he'd been killed by their headman. She took great pleasure in revealing to me that, after his death, all his property went to her. As such I'd become her slave."

"*Mon Dieu.*" Mariena came to him and took hold of his hand. "Was there nothing you could do to put an end to that?"

"'Twas my end, I reckoned, for she'd wished me dead since my birth. As her slave I'd no more rights or protection than a cow or a field of oats. She could kill me at her whim." Her touch made it a little easier to continue with the dreadful recollection. "Only Sileas said she'd already disposed of me. She'd send me as a gift to the Carrack, to serve their headman."

"She gave you to the man who killed your father?" Mariena looked horrified now. "Was she insane? No, don't answer. I know she was."

"'Twas part of a truce she parlayed. She traded me as a bed slave for a promise of peace between the tribes." After all the centuries that had passed the old anger and horror felt thin and distant, like ghosts that came only to haunt his nightmares. "I'd no desire to lay with another man, but 'twasnae the worst. I'd heard the whispers about my new master. 'Twas said that he bedded only young male slaves, and wasnae particularly gentle with them. To escape his cruel lusts in the end many opened their veins, or jumped from the ridges."

"That *putain* didn't care about peace." Mariena's eyes took on a lethal calmness. "She did this to see you suffer."

"Aye, and her scheme, 'twas well-reckoned as 'twas vicious. She assured that I'd live out the rest of my days as my *máthair* had, a bed slave. Since the Carrack headman favored the handsome, she predicted I'd be facked every night." He gripped her hand a little tighter. "To ken I'd be used by the same brute who had killed my sire, mayhap 'twas her revenge on us both."

Her fingers twined through his. "Did you run away?"

Broden had long imagined what life would have been like for the Mag Raith if he had. "No," he said gazing down at their hands before looking into her eyes. "I said I'd go, as befit a slave."

"You what?" Her fingers tightened around his.

"I saw how to make a trap of myself for Sileas and my tribe. For enslaving my *máthair*, for throttling me, for sending me away, for using me to protect themselves—for every misery I'd suffered in my worthless life—I'd end them all." He released her hand. "I had only to seduce a brute, murder him in his bed, and declare to his tribe that I'd been sent to kill him."

Understanding came into her eyes. "Oh, no."

"I reckoned every detail. How to smuggle in the dagger. What I'd do to get behind my new master. Ending him by cutting his throat, to keep him quiet. All the terrible ways I'd despoil his body. I'd wait until the Carrack's men found me beside their dead leader. Before I buried a blade in my heart, I'd claim Sileas sent me no' as a slave to make peace, but as her assassin to avenge her mate."

"You would take your revenge by making them think it hers," Mariena said, her voice shaking a little. "It was as perfect as what she had planned for you."

"No other Pritani tribe could match the Carrack for their savagery. I reckoned my lie, 'twould inflame them beyond all reason." Broden felt empty now, as if he'd whittled out his insides. "They wouldnae rest until they'd hunted and killed every member of my sire's tribe. Yet Sileas I suspected they'd take alive. They'd want to cause her as much suffering as she could endure. She, a helpless female, and yet I had no pity for her. I wanted her to ken agony, and die a ravaged ruin."

"Just as she wished for you. Wait." Her brows drew together. "You went on that hunt with your brothers, no? And this was when you were taken by the demons?" When he nodded she uttered a long sigh. "You tell me these terrible things as if you did them. The Sluath captured you before you could go to the Carrack."

"'Twas all that saved Sileas and my tribe from my death trap." Broden smiled a little. "The Gods knew my black heart, and so did the Sluath. I'm the reason the demons took the Mag Raith. They came for me. All we've suffered, 'twas my doing."

❧

A WISP of thistle down drifted in through the window and floated between Mariena and Broden. She watched it move through the air as she tried to think of what to say to him. She didn't understand his beliefs, but she'd heard the conviction in his voice as he'd blamed himself for their capture. Since she shared the same terrible suspicion about herself, she knew nothing would likely change his dark view. She might have done the same, or worse. Likely worse, if her instincts were anything to judge her former life by.

Mariena also understood that hopelessness of being caught between a terrible past and an unknowable future. She might never know the truth of who she had been, and what she had done, but she knew her capabilities. She didn't have to see the blood on her hands to know it was there. One did not become a killer by accident. Yet Nellie's candor about her own terrible past had persuaded her to think differently.

Whatever you were before, that's done. You can't

change it, or go back to your time. What you can do is make a new life here.

Now, somehow, she had to make Broden understand that.

Reaching out to touch the scar Sileas had left on him, Mariena felt her lover flinch. "The night I came here, I held a dagger to your throat. If your clan had tried to hurt me, I would have used it. You had done nothing to me, and I would have killed you. Our hearts, they are the same, *mon charmant*."

His mouth thinned. "You defended yourself against strangers. I meant to slaughter a tribe. My tribe. Old ones, young lads, mothers, bairns."

"You did not slaughter them, and no one can say what you would have done. You might have changed your mind, gotten free, run away. Or someone who cared might have helped you escape." Suddenly she thought of the other men of the clan. She had seen how close they were, and all of them treated Broden as they did each other, as family. "Before she left with you, Sileas would have told the hunters, no?"

His expression darkened. "Aye, she took particular pleasure in shaming me thus."

"Just so. I think Domnall and the others, they

would do nothing to help you." She pretended not to see his startled look as she tapped a finger against her chin. "She knew that."

"I belonged to Sileas as her property, my lady." He sounded as if she'd punched him in the belly. "'Twas naught they could have done for a slave."

"No, I think she wouldn't worry. She knew they would not care. She was so sure that she let you hunt with them." She made a sweeping gesture. "I know they called you their brother, but they did not mean it. You don't share the bloodline, and among your people, that is what counts, no?"

Broden scowled. "You dinnae ken my brothers."

"Do you? Once they learned that Sileas had made you a brute's sex slave, perhaps they would have been glad to be rid of you? To never hunt with you again? They must have thought you deserved such a terrible fate for being..." She stopped and peered at him. "Too handsome? No, they don't seem to resent your perfect face and body. Your poor hunting skills, then...only they think you are the best trapper in Scotland. Hmmm." She smiled. "Well, there is your voice. It is far from perfect. Maybe they despised you for that."

Broden looked so dumbstruck she would not have been surprised to see him drop in a heap. "I never reckoned they'd care what became of me."

"Then you are still blind, and not so very clever." She closed the distance between them and wrapped her arms around his neck. "Why do I sleep with you? I could do much better." Gently she pulled him close and murmured against his ear. "Now, you listen to me, *mon ange*. This is what I can promise you: Domnall and the others, they would never have allowed you to go to that terrible headman. They would have taken you away from Sileas. They love you, as you love them." *As I love you*, she added silently.

"I'm no' so noble as my brothers," he said into her hair. "Since we escaped the underworld, I've never told them of the vengeance I'd planned."

She knew that her power could not heal this terrible unseen wound in him, but she suspected revealing his secrets would. Yet that would have to be his choice.

"Whatever you choose to tell your clan, that part of your life is gone, *mon charmant*. You can never go back and change the wrathful man you were. You survived Sileas, and the Sluath, and now you are here. You must live as the fine man you have become." She felt him tremble and turned her face so she could kiss his. "My very handsome, skilled man with the terrible voice."

Silently he held her until his shaking stopped. He didn't weep, but when he drew back she saw a line of blood on his bottom lip where he'd bitten it. Gently she brushed her fingers over the small wound, and grimaced as she tasted blood.

"My thanks, my lady," he said.

"I'm glad you told me," she said, looking down. Mariena suspected Broden was in no state for more unnerving revelations, so she turned away and headed for the door. "I promised the chieftain I would explore all the castle today. There is much more to look at, no?"

"I ken your secret," Broden said, stopping her. "You took Nellie's arrow wounds from her back after the battle. You healed my neck, my knee, and even my eyes. You've a power that takes injuries from others, and makes them yours."

She tensed for a moment and then her shoulders sagged. Her carelessness had not gone unnoticed. But of course, how could it not? Had she secretly wanted him to know?

"Yes," she finally said. "I have only to touch the injuries."

"You blinded yourself for me." He turned her around to face him, a scowl deeply furrowing his brow. "How could you be so reckless? Did you ken you would heal?"

"I always do." Mariena shrugged. "Very well. The next time you are blinded, I will not touch you."

Broden's grip gentled. "Tell me why you kept your power a secret."

"I made a promise. The demon who helped us escape sent me here on a mission, but I cannot remember it." She saw how his muscles tensed, making his inked glyphs bulge. "There is more I have kept secret. The demon also gave us our powers, and Dun Chaill did not save the women of your clan. The tattoos on their bodies brought them back to life."

He released her. "How?"

"I don't know that," she admitted. "The demon told me that mortal slaves were marked so they could be brought back and made immortal, but only by their Sluath masters in the underworld. All I can tell you is that it should not have happened here."

Broden rubbed his brow. "We must find Domnall, and go to the forge."

Mariena followed him out of the room. "If we are to tell your chieftain, we should bring the others." She heard a sound from the other end of the passage and turned to see a tall, figure watching them. "Broden."

Fury filled his eyes. "Galan, you fack."

The tall man bared his teeth in a horrible smile, and then fled into the tower.

Chapter Twenty-Four

PRINCE IOLAR EMERGED from the dismal cottage he occupied, startling the two demons standing guard. He ignored them as he scanned the horizon. He saw no storms approaching, but felt again the trace of power that had stirred him from his lethargy. The stench of the mortals he'd butchered in the night crept out to envelop him. While it was his favorite perfume, it also stoked the hunger he could no longer assuage.

In the underworld Iolar abided far more comfortably in his father's towering manse of snow-white stone. Once staffed by dozens of humans the king had personally trained—and Iolar had later gleefully butchered—it had contained every priceless treasure His Majesty had filched from the time stream.

A stunning number of useless objects had cluttered the place. Bowls of diamonds, some as big as Danar's fist, had sat beside chests of gold and pearls. Tapestries embroidered with rare silks that depicted fantastic creatures once covered the walls. One room alone had been packed with scrolls taken from some infamous library in Alexandria before it had been burned. As soon as the king and his retainers had died miserably, Iolar had ordered the demons loyal to him to help themselves to whatever they liked. It had been the easiest way to clear out the damn place. The scrolls he'd burned, one by one, imagining how the king would have screamed to see such wanton destruction of his precious mortal scribblings.

The one treasure Iolar had kept for himself, the one every demon still coveted, had provided him with all the pleasure he could ever desire.

"I should have taken Nellie Quinn," he said, almost feeling wistful now. "She would have told me where she hid my treasure." And if she hadn't, he still might have amused himself with her.

A large silhouette blocked out the sun.

"My prince." Danar bowed. "How may I serve?"

"Send someone to clean out this hovel," he told the big demon. "It's beginning to stink of rotting corpses. Oh, and take out the rotting corpses first." He noticed something as he glanced around the village to select the next candidates for his amusement. "Where are the village idiots?"

Danar nodded toward the mess inside his cottage. "Those you took were the last of our stocks, my liege. Galan promised to procure more for your needs, but he has not yet returned from the Emerald Glen."

Iolar doubted Galan would. "Then you must do it. Make sure that they're young and strong. I don't want any more gnarled old men or their cross-eyed crones." He eyed him. "Why are you still standing here?"

The big demon bowed and trotted off.

Iolar walked through the village, aware that every guard and sentry watched him with open fear and barely-concealed anger. The longer the Sluath remained stranded in the mortal realm, the more they hungered for the pleasures of the underworld. Although they were immortal and couldn't literally starve, neither could they sustain themselves here. To thrive as they were, they needed to cull souls they could enslave.

Soon some of the stronger, more malicious demons would challenge him for rule. Iolar could prevail over a few, but he had depleted his power twice now. If enough banded together against him he would end as his father had, skewered to his throne by iron and slowly decapitated.

"Ah, the good old days," he murmured fondly. He had enjoyed sawing off the old bastard's fat head, and placing it on a pike in the center of the slave arena, so the rest of the demons could watch it slowly shrivel into twisted ash.

That had set the perfect note for Iolar's coronation gala.

In those days the supply of mortals had been a constant deluge, thanks to the savagery rampant in the mortal realm. Iolar could remember times when he'd culled a thousand souls at once, returning to the underworld during the same storm he'd used to hunt them. The Mongols in particular had provided so many tasty delights. From their time the Sluath had culled so many slaves they'd had to suspend most of them in ice.

Thanks to the inherent inanity of mortals there would always be wars and genocides and plagues enough to keep the demons well-supplied. Yet those glory days of taking as many souls as the Sluath wanted were gone. They could use the time stream to move through the millennia, but it never allowed them to revisit a time in the past or future that they'd already culled. The only exception was this time in Scotland, a mystery that the king had never explained to him.

At the edge of the village Iolar sniffed the air until he caught the scent of the diminutive source. As he expected it stank of child and druid. He followed it into the forest, where he spied a young boy sitting in the oak tree.

It seemed his grand plan had been a success. "You're late."

"Forgive me, my prince. I had to change several times." The druid toddler jumped from the branch to the ground, where he gazed up at Iolar with soft, innocent eyes. "Everything went exactly as you wished."

The prince smelled fear and bared his teeth. "Convince me of that."

"I persuaded the idiots of the Emerald Glen tribe to give me to Galan when he came looking for Druman," the boy said. "It wasn't at all as difficult as I'd imagined. That Bhaltair Flen fellow must instill terror wherever he goes. Also, I pulled the vision of the boy out of their minds with no effort. We should consider trying to cull—oh, but he's a druid. Never mind."

Rolling his hand kept the prince from lunging and tearing out the boy's thin throat.

"Yes, well, Galan stole me from them, as he'd promised you. He never tried to come here, however. He took me as his hostage to the ruins of an ancient settlement. It smelled of those bones he brought back for you to resurrect." The boy showed his little teeth in a wide smile. "There he tormented me, but only a little, and demanded I tell him about the disappearance of the Mag Raith and their tribe. As you commanded, I told him what we know."

Iolar felt the first pleasure of his day. Stirring the druid's madness into a froth had become a little game for him—Galan made it remarkably easy, too—but the real work had been awakening what lay dormant inside him. That had required very careful calculation.

"Where is Galan now?" he demanded.

"I can't tell you, my prince." The boy took a wary step back. "He disappeared just outside the settlement. He also took with him what was left of his spies."

Pleasure, as usual, became fleeting. "You let him get away?"

As Iolar came at the boy he dropped and prostrated himself in the leaf rot. "Please, my liege. I could not follow him. He sent me to look for myself, and he'd never believe I was one of his spies. I thought it more important to keep him from discovering my subterfuge."

Iolar raised his claws. Tempting as it was to shove a bolt of power through the bumbling idiot, he'd actually done far better than expected. After waiting long enough to taste his fear, he slapped his hand atop the small head, and drew from the demon the power he'd lent him so he could retain his shift-forms longer and disguise his scent.

Seabhag instantly changed from the druid boy to a helpless-looking young mortal female. "Forgive me, my prince. I could not risk ruining your plan–"

"Stop cowering, fool. If I wanted you dead, I'd have already torn you to pieces." Iolar turned away, sighing with pleasure as his increased power surged through him. "What did you do with the real druid brat?"

"I fully intended to bring him as a gift for you." Seabhag cautiously rose to his feet. "But when I arrived at the settlement, Druman had already been taken away. They wouldn't tell me where, but once I killed a few of them, they agreed to help me convince Galan I was the child." His pretty face took on an uneasy expression. "It was a little odd, how cooperative they were. They didn't expect me, of course, but I think they knew the mad druid was coming for the boy. I just don't know how."

Iolar had never liked druids, who died as strangely as they lived, and this last revelation unsettled him. But Galan's people could never do anything to harm him or his demons, so it didn't really matter. "Come. We must speak to Danar about preparing for Galan's return."

Seabhag shifted into a skinny old man and trotted alongside him. "Why should the druid come back to us, my prince?"

"Clamhan is better at following him than you," Iolar assured him. "That's how he found out where the druid hid his wretched wife's bones. If Galan wants his precious Fiana, then he'll have to come to me and ask nicely for them."

Chapter Twenty-Five

BRODEN WENT BACK into his chamber, and with a jerk ripped apart the rope holding his trunk out of reach. Catching it as it dropped, he tore open the lid, took out their blades and handed Mariena's to her.

"This Galan, he's the druid who serves the demons now?" she asked as she strapped on her sword and tucked away her daggers. "The one who hurt Kiaran, and tried to kill all the women of the clan?"

"Aye, he's that fack," he told her. "We cannae permit him leave Dun Chaill. He'll lead the Sluath back to us."

"Ah, so then he dies before he can. Simple." Mariena glanced at him. "Aren't you going to tell me to stay here and be safe while you go and hunt him?"

"You can protect yourself, my lady," he told her. "While I'm safer with you at my side."

Her lips curved. "I love you."

They rushed out into the passage, and ran to the arch leading into the rebuilt tower. Before they entered she made the clan's signal for silence and drew her dagger. When Broden indicated they should ascend in diagonal flanking positions, she moved slightly ahead of his own to take lead.

Galan had extinguished the tower's torches, leaving them to smolder in his wake. Broden eyed the tracks he'd left in the dust on the stone steps. They lead straight up, but were smudged, as if he had retraced his steps. Broden turned in the darkness as he examined the walls, and felt a tendril of air against his face. Stepping in that direction, he saw the curve of the outer wall, which Jenna had just rebuilt.

The center of the stones had been blasted out, allowing the *dru-wid* to escape the tower.

Like an experienced siege warrior Mariena kept her back to the wall as she approached the opening, her gaze fixed on the darkness beyond it.

She stopped and tilted her head to peer inside, and then glanced at Broden and shrugged.

Picking up one of the fallen stones, he hurled it through the gap. He heard it strike more stone and roll away.

Before he could go through, Mariena darted inside the opening, her blade ready as she shifted to one side. Broden followed and mirrored her position as he scanned the interior.

They had come into a chamber, not the passage on the other side of the tower. The one torch burning inside showed sloping stone walls surrounding an odd floor of dark wood that had been cut with deep channels filled with some murky liquid. The pitted walls appeared to be fashioned from single boulders hewn in enormous rounds. Over time they had tilted, and now leaned against each other at the top to form an irregular peak. On the floor beneath the peak stood a narrow pyramid-shaped altar of sorts, fashioned from thin wood staves. Atop the altar a small, dark bronze sphere had been placed.

Broden didn't know if it was a sacred place—he'd never seen the like made by *dru-wid* or Pritani tribes—but something about the chamber gave him pause. It felt as if he should know its purpose, yet he couldn't fathom it.

He circled around to the back of the altar, but found no exit to the chamber. As he lifted his free hand to give Mariena the signal to retreat he saw another stone hurl in through the opening. It smashed through the pyramid, sending the bronze sphere whirling into the air. Instead of falling it kept rising, attaching itself to the center of where the stones met, where it began to glow with amber light.

A heavy stone panel abruptly dropped down over the opening, sealing them inside.

"'Tis another trap," Broden said as he strode over to grab the panel and move it aside. The moment he touched it a jolt of power slammed into him, and hurled him across the chamber. As he slid down and fell to his knees, crackling blue light swept over the panel.

Mariena came to him as he stood, and reached out, pressing her hand to his chest. She frowned. "You're not injured."

"Aye, but I barely touched it." The sound of stones scraping together over their heads made him glance up at the peak, and then at the surrounding sloped stones. "Fack the Gods."

The chamber appeared to be shrinking, with the walls slowly sliding toward the inside. The stones turned as they slid on the strange channels on the floor which met directly in the center, where the pyramid had stood. Broden saw a pale dust sifting down through the air, and smelled the must of old grain. He then understood why the place had seemed so familiar.

"The walls are moving in on us," Mariena said, aghast. "What sort of chamber is this?"

"No' a chamber," Broden said as he pulled her into the center. "'Twas once the castle's mill-house. The watcher bespelled it as a trap. Disturbing the sphere triggered it to grind anything that came within the stones."

"That would be us." She looked at the panel blocking their only exit, and her expression darkened. "I will not wait to be crushed to death."

He didn't know what she meant until she strode toward the panel. "Mariena, no." He ran after her, but he couldn't reach her before she touched the enchanted stone.

❧

THE UNHOLY BLUE fire that enveloped Mariena

burned through her as it hurled her back, not into Broden's arm but into the labyrinth of her own memories. She sensed what was coming, and writhed and fought the forces tearing at her. They ignored her struggles and dragged her through time to the last night she'd spent in Paris.

Climbing off her bicycle outside 84 Avenue Foch, Mariena squinted against the flinty wind. The wooden soles of her shoes clocked against the pavement while she straightened her long skirt and patched pinafore. At any other spot in Paris she would have padlocked her precious bike to the nearest fence, for thievery had grown rampant as petrol supplies had dwindled, but not here.

No one, not even the most desperate of black market thieves, stole from Gestapo Headquarters.

From the bike's front basket, she took the sack containing Russian caviar and Krug champagne for the SS Commander whose offices she cleaned each week. The major believed she had access to the forbidden goods through a non-existent criminal brother. Obtaining such delicacies, now scarce in the third year of the occupation, helped her keep her job while most of Paris was out of work. Since she also spoke passable German, the major didn't have to use one of his translators to relay his orders to her.

Mariena thought of her own dinner: a slice of stale bread and a half-cup of lukewarm black chicory coffee. After two days of having nothing to eat it had seemed like a feast.

The two guards flanking the side entryway shifted their hands to their sidearms as she approached. Once she drew close enough to be recognized they relaxed again. She felt their gazes crawling over her evening uniform, but not in suspicion.

While shabby and old, Mariena's uniform had been expertly tailored to fit the padding that doubled the size of her breasts, belly and hips. The Germans barely glanced at her face, hidden as it was under a layer of thick, pitted pancake makeup in an unflattering shade of ochre. The frilled cap, brown wig and spectacles completed the illusion of a plump, unremarkable maid with bad skin.

"Guten abend, Herren," Mariena murmured as she stopped and held out the sack for the usual inspection.

"Don't bother," the one guard said to the other when he reached for it. "She buys special fripperies for the major." He opened the door for her. "Hurry along, little drab. He's in no mood to wait tonight."

Once inside the old villa Mariena made her way up the creaking stairs. On the third floor landing the commander's security men, always suspicious of everyone, stopped her and checked her sack. When the muffled sounds of weeping and begging came from the corridor behind them, she ducked her head and let her hands tremble. Feigning fear while hiding her rage had become second nature since *la patronne* had sent her into the Occupied Zone.

"Is that the maid?" a hard voice called from above them. "Send her to me now."

Mariena quickly climbed up to the fourth floor, where the short, rotund figure of the commander paced back and forth. He snatched the sack from her hands and gestured for her to follow him into his office.

"You must be quick tonight, girl," the major told her, and pointed to the top of his usually immaculate desk, which now had been covered in cat hair. "Everything is to be made pristine by the time I return with the *Hauptsturmführer*, you understand?"

Dutifully Mariena bobbed and went to retrieve her cleaning supplies from the adjacent closet. As soon as she heard the door open and close again, she dropped a rag, and bent over to retrieve it. With practiced ease she slid out the thin blade hidden in the wooden sole of her shoe, and saw her face reflected by the blade.

Her eyes made some people nervous. Partly blue, like her father's, they had patches of her mother's golden-brown irises. It occurred to her that she hadn't looked in a mirror since her parents and grandparents had fled Paris with a Jewish friend's young daughter, to whom Mariena had lent her papers. Her eyes reminded her of just how much had been taken from her. Though her parents had intended to return for her, her entire family had been bombed out of existence by a Luftwaffe strafing attack.

The Nazis hadn't just murdered everyone she loved. They'd killed her, too.

Being declared dead along with the rest of the Douets had destroyed more than Mariena's identity. She'd lost her home, her father's practice, all of her inheritance, and every scrap of hope she'd had for the future. She couldn't go back to medical school. She had no papers, and hardly any money. None of her well-off friends or their families had stayed in the city after the occupation. Those too poor to flee had nothing to offer her, or had become collaborators who could not be trusted.

All Mariena had left was her rage, and nothing could take that from her—not joining the resistance, not being trained as a courier, not even when a drunken Nazi had attacked and tried to rape her in the shadow of the Arc de Triomphe. While he had been tearing at her clothes, she'd yanked the dress dagger from his belt.

Killing him had required only a single, precise jab.

Mariena watched him bleed out from the carotid she'd severed in his neck before she'd walked away, the dripping blade still clutched in her hand. Somehow she found her way into a darkened alley. Leaning against the ancient bricks, she had waited to be sick, to hate herself. Instead she felt as calm as she had the first time she had picked up a scalpel in medical school. She lifted the blade and studied the open-winged eagle on the crossguard. It clutched a wreathed swastika in its talons, as sure as the Nazis now held Paris.

After she reported what she had done, the

leader of the Alliance had offered to smuggle her out of France. When Mariena refused, Poz had suggested she do something other than carry messages.

"I don't want more training," Mariena had said as she handed him the Nazi's dagger. "But I will need a clean blade."

Now sliding the stiletto into her sleeve ended Mariena's reverie. She took her feather duster and went to attend to the major's desk, stopping when she saw the man waiting on the other side. Short and average-looking, his thin slash of a mouth seemed as flat as his pale gunmetal eyes. He wasn't in uniform, but she knew exactly who he was.

Her target, come to her.

How obliging of him.

"Marie-Anne, is it?" the Butcher of Lyon asked in French distorted by his German accent. "Josef mentioned he'd hired a maid from the hotel down the street."

"Bien sûr, Monsieur." Mariena looked at the small kitten he held cradled against his chest, unable to make her mouth curve into the expected smile. In German she said, "Such a pretty cat. Is this your first visit to Paris?"

"No." He placed the kitten atop the desk, where it walked over to sniff at the duster in her hand. "I came so that I might meet a very special visitor. Perhaps the major mentioned this?"

Mariena knew several *resistants* had been captured within the past weeks. All but one had been brought to 84 Avenue Foch before being shipped to the prison at Kehl. *La patronne* had hoped that the missing man had either escaped or been killed in the attempt, for he was very high-ranked and knew too much about the resistance. If Mariena discovered the agent at Gestapo Headquarters, she was to deal with him, too.

"No, Monsieur." She stroked the little cat's back, making it arch against her palm. "The commander only spoke of you."

"I came to meet a resistance agent code named *Le Cygne*. You have heard of this one? No?" He made a chiding sound. "Quite the legend now. We have confirmed twenty-eight murders of my countrymen by this agent over the last two years. That's more than one every month. A remarkable achievement for a lone killer, don't you think?"

"I cannot tell you, Monsieur."

Mariena shrugged as she moved around the

desk, luring the kitten along with the movement of the duster. At the same time she twisted her other wrist to settle the hilt of her blade into her palm.

Betrayal had become a problem for the Alliance since the Gestapo had begun torturing the agents they captured. In Mariena's head she heard again what the *la patronne* had told her when she had stopped being a courier and had become their most effective assassin.

Le Cygne *must never be caught,* ma chére amie.

"We Germans have a fault of being too literal," the Butcher continued. "The word for swan in French is in the male form—*le cygne*. Yet who else but a man with military expertise could slay so many of our well-trained soldiers? Surely, he must be an older fellow. Perhaps a veteran of the First World War."

"Have you captured him, then, sir?" Mariena asked, watching the kitten as it pounced on the duster, and discreetly shifting into the best position to reach his throat.

The Nazi chuckled. "I believe we have, Marie-Anne."

A heartbeat passed, and she felt the air behind her move. Pain crashed down on her neck, blazing through her spine. Then darkness swallowed the kitten and the office and the Butcher of Lyon, and finally her.

Mariena roused some time later, her body contorted in a strange and painful position. Her arms stretched high above her head, her body and feet dangling. She could feel coldness on her naked skin, and the sound of someone whistling softly, cheerfully. A hissing sound sliced through the air by her ear, and a lash of fire licked over her shoulder and back.

"Not yet, Major." The Butcher stepped out of the shadows, the kitten back in his arms as he peered up at her. "She's only just awakened. We must allow this poor creature a moment to collect herself. She may wish to bargain with us. So many do when they come to this room."

"The bitch used me in hopes of murdering you, Captain," the commander said as he came around to face her. "I want to watch her writhe under my whip until she weeps blood."

His flushed face and fish-scented breath told her how to reply.

"Then you'd better hurry and do it," Mariena told him. "I poisoned the food and the wine. Your guts will start melting from the acid any moment now."

The major blanched and then dropped the whip and ran from the room, shouting for the doctor who attended to the prisoners.

"Very good, Marie-Anne," the Butcher said, laughing. "I must remember to try such a ruse when I return to Lyon."

"I've been cleaning this pig sty for weeks," she told him. "Including the kitchens and the pantry. Did you eat well tonight, *Boche*?"

"If you wish to frighten me, my dear, you must do better than that." He produced her blade, parking the tip just beneath her chin. "I know your weapon of choice is not poison."

"You know nothing about me," Mariena told him, and made a show of yawning. "Nor will you, so finish it. I'm tired of looking at your stupid face."

"A quick jab to the carotid, the femoral artery, or directly into the heart, and your victims are dead in a few minutes," the Butcher continued. "How did you acquire such excellent knowledge of anatomy? Were you a nurse, perhaps, or did someone in particular in Noah's Ark tutor you? Poz, your esteemed leader? You could give me that wretch's real identity, and perhaps save your own hide."

She spat at him, but her mouth was too dry and produced nothing.

"I found these in your apron." He reached into his pocket and took out a packet of white tablets. "A pity you didn't reach for them instead of your blade. Potassium cyanide isn't a pleasant end, but it's quicker than any I'll choose to give you."

She'd brought the poison to give it to the captured agent, but that no longer concerned her. Looking into the lifeless charcoal of his eyes, Mariena saw her fate. She would never leave this room again. An expert in torture, the Butcher would fill the remainder of her days with excruciating agony. Her only hope lay in goading him.

"I am only the first sent for you, *Boche*," she told him. "Poz has legions waiting for a chance at you. He will have them waiting outside, on the road back to Lyon, at the Hôtel Terminus, in your suite, in your bed–"

The Nazi drove the stiletto into her thigh, ramming it in until it glanced off her bone. He uttered a grunt of satisfaction as he jerked it out. Blood poured from the wound, but did not spurt.

"You missed," she taunted him. "Three inches over for the artery, *imbécile.*"

"I'm wearing my last clean uniform, and you are not going to die so quickly." He lifted the thin blade and wiped it clean on her cheek. "Do you know what I did last week?"

She arched her brows. "Before or after you licked your Fuhrer's ass? But you do this every day. It must take up so much of your time."

He scraped some of the makeup from her cheek, frowning as a sculptor would at his work. "You have lovely skin."

"You don't," she assured him.

"Last week I skinned a man alive, and then I drowned him in ammonia. Carefully he plied the stiletto to the other side of her face. "I made his children watch every moment of his torment."

"Why do you think they sent me for you?" Mariena countered, sniffing back the hot looseness rushing into her eyes and nose. "Because you smell like an overfull privy? Well, that, too."

"Have you ever been forced to drink from a privy bucket? We make the sentries use them." His thin lips spread into a ghastly grin as he backed away from her. "Rest now, Marie-Anne. When I return, you can give me more suggestions for our first session. I hope you're thirsty."

He walked out, letting the door swing slowly closed behind him. Mariena tilted her face up to study the way she'd been tied to the chain hoist holding her suspended. The thick rope had been knotted tightly, and the ends tucked up out of reach of her fingers. Already her hands had gone numb and white from lack of circulation. In another hour she'd lose all use of them.

Beneath her and around her lay nothing. All the furnishings had been removed from the room. Soon the Butcher would return with some guards who would use whips, and cudgels and maces to beat her. She knew how she could goad the soldiers into being more violent with her, perhaps even to the point of losing control and killing her quickly. But first, she had to make herself weaker, and that meant taking advantage of what the Butcher had already done.

Slowly Mariena lifted her wounded leg, bunching her thigh and hissing with pain as she watched the flow from the puncture. More flexing increased the bleeding. Through the tears of pain in her eyes she saw a small puddle forming on the floor beneath her.

The door swung open, and the Butcher stepped back inside. He looked around the room before he focused on her face. His features shimmered until she blinked away the tears.

"Are your men afraid of a cleaning woman?" Mariena demanded. "Not that this would shock me."

He said nothing to her as he walked around her, and then opened the window behind her. As the cold night air rushed over her throbbing back she heard a strange sound, like something digging into wood. The Nazi then came back around her, sniffing at her like a dog before drawing back and scowling.

"Still righteous," he muttered under his breath, but in a deeper, harder voice with no German accent at all. "With all the blood on your hands I thought for certain…but no matter. I can still use you." He grinned at her, and his teeth shifted in his mouth, growing long and jagged, like an animal's. "Yes, one look and he'll be ready to defile all that lovely snowy flesh."

Mariena's arms riddled with goosebumps. "What are you?"

The thing that was not the Butcher suddenly grew six-inch claws and swiped at the chain suspending her. Mariena screamed as she fell heavily to the floor. The impact sent a bolt of pain through her injured leg and knocked the breath out of her lungs, and still she managed to roll over and stagger to her feet.

The Butcher's body writhed and changed shape into something huge and beautiful and ghastly, its wings spreading out in glittering glory as it stalked toward her.

Mariena turned and ran for the open window, praying her fall would be enough to kill her. But icy claws snatched her back and threw her to the floor.

The gold and white creature that straddled her began to shimmer into another shape as it raised its claws. "This should shock you."

She didn't understand until he thrust his claws into her chest, and curled them around her heart.

Chapter Twenty-Six

THE RUMBLE OF the grinding stones shifting came through the passages, sending dust down on Cul's head. Someone had triggered the mill trap. At the same time, he could sense Galan, so close now that only a few walls separated them. But the druid was moving away from the crushing trap, which meant one or more of the intruders had entered and activated the killing spell.

Mariena and Broden had been the closest to the mill room.

Cul summoned two of the iron warriors guarding the tunnels and sent them to shadow the druid. Ordering them to kill him would have given him more satisfaction, but Iolar's pet might be more useful to him alive. He had the sense that all he had worked toward was swiftly coming to fruition. He would not waste centuries of planning for a few moments of pleasure.

He turned and hobbled back toward the tower. If Mariena died between the mill stones, she would not resurrect—and his twisted limbs would not be healed. He reached for the wall and summoned his power.

"I will keep my promise, little slave."

❧

BRODEN KEPT his arms braced against the mill's walls as he watched Mariena stirring. Holding the collapsing stones apart had required all of his strength, but he knew he couldn't hold them indefinitely. Every power had limits, and doubtless his would fail him in time. Long before that, however, the crushing pressure of the giant wheels would splinter the bones in his arms.

"My lady." He could barely hear himself above the churning grate. "Come back to me now."

Mariena opened her eyes, and looked at him as she pressed a hand over her heart. Her eyes widened as she took in his stance, and she scrambled to her feet. She turned around, taking in the scant amount of space left to them before she faced him again.

"Your tattoo, it has turned silver," she said as she tried to smile.

Broden glanced at his marked arm. "So 'twould seem."

"I remember my life. Now I am going to try to forget it again." Mariena lifted the edge of her tunic to look at her skinwork. "My ink has gone silver, too. We are going to die here, no? So, I will tell you again: I love you. I would tell you other things, but they are better in French."

"You shall live," he told her, and swallowed a groan as the pressure of the contracting stones increased. "We've still time. I'll pull away the panel blocking the opening, and you shall squeeze through."

"That did not go so well the last time. It will burn off your face, and then I will die sad as well as squashed." She crouched down and looked at the bottoms of the stones, and then tilted her head back. "The stones, they began to move after that metal ball flew to the top, no? And that is where the grain poured in."

"Aye." He followed the direction of her gaze

and saw where the bronze sphere had attached itself. It lay only an arm's length from the top of his head now.

"If I take it down," she said, "perhaps the wheels will stop moving."

Broden nodded. "Climb on me. Stand on my shoulders."

Mariena hoisted herself up on him, bracing her knees on either side of his neck. "I have noticed that you will not say you love me. So now I must be honest, too. I lied both times. I love your hair more than you."

"Every lass tells me that," he said through his clenched teeth. "You may shave my head once we're clear."

"No. I want you to grow it longer so I can wear it like a scarf." She straightened, her belly grazing his face as she reached up. "Don't worry. I will be naked and in your bed when I do this. Almost there, *mon charmant*."

Broden felt his arms beginning to tremble, and pitted all of his strength against the stones. Mariena vaulted off of him, the sphere in her hand, and the walls stopped moving. Slowly the panel rose, revealing the opening. At the same time the enormous mill stones began to shudder as cracks streaked through them.

She looked at him. "We should run very fast now."

Broden released the walls, scooping her up in his sweat-slick arms as he raced for the opening. He felt the whole chamber shudder as he jumped through to the outside, and the tremendous crash of the crumbling stones as they collapsed. A cloud of dust and gravel billowed out, enveloping them. The relief of having escaped the trap warred inside him with the deadly fury he felt toward the *dru-wid*.

"Merde alors." Mariena buried her face against his neck. "I am killing this Galan, as soon as I stop shaking."

"Fack the *dru-wid*. Look at me." When she lifted her head he kissed her, hard and fast. "Naught touches the hair…but you, *a thasgaidh*. I love you."

Her eyes lit up with so much love it seemed to spill out of her like light. "You could not mention this when we were dying in the crushing trap? For someone who loves me you are very cruel. What if we had died?"

"We shall live, my lady." Broden kissed her

again, and then looked over her head as Domnall and Mael rushed into the tower, their swords ready. "'Tis Galan," he told his brothers. "He's found us."

The seneschal swore as the chieftain took in the haze and rubble around them.

"I shall summon the others," Domnall said. "We cannae permit him escape." He lifted a carved wooden reed hanging from a thong around his neck to his lips, and used it to blast three shrill whistles that echoed through the passage.

"Bravo." Mariena grinned with delight. "Did you make one for me?"

Chapter Twenty-Seven

THE SOUND OF the collapsing mill made Galan chuckle as he hurried out of the stronghold. Luring Broden and his slut into the trap had been ridiculously simple. Although he felt tempted to remain in the keepe and deal with the rest of the Mag Raith, he had to find where Culvar now hid himself.

Outside the sunlight briefly dazzled his eyes, and then something struck and tore at his face with sharp claws as it shrieked. Galan swore as he tried to seize the kestrel, but the raptor eluded him, and soared back up into the sky. Wiping the blood from his eyes, he saw it join six others hovering out of reach. All the cursed birds then began shrieking loudly. He hurled a bolt of power at them, but they quickly scattered.

"Aedth." The sun set Edane mag Raith's hair ablaze as he appeared atop the curtain wall. He jumped and landed a short distance away, an arrow notched in his bow. "By the Gods, I've longed for this day."

"I havenae missed you, weakling," Galan taunted. He drew on his power, allowing it to suffuse him as he spread his arms. "Aye, shoot me again. Your slut isnae here to protect you now."

Galan's smile faded as he saw Domnall and Mael come out into the light, and Kiaran appear on his other side. Their wenches, each armed, spread out behind them.

"Hold." Broden came striding out of the tower arch, his hair and body covered in gray dust and a gleaming sword in his fist. "He's mine."

"Unless I reach him first, *mon ange*," the equally grubby mortal female at his side said, blades in both hands.

Galan knew he might easily prevail over the sluts, but Broden's strength combined with the other Mag Raith and their talents was too much for him. He spat on the ground before he turned and ran into the forest, heading for the river. At the same time, he sent out a command to his mortal spies, and heard them dropping from the trees all around him.

A blur streaked past him, solidifying into Domnall, who stopped and folded his arms as he blocked his path. "You cannae run from us, coward. 'Tis time you answer for all the evil you've done."

Galan lifted his glowing hands and blasted the big man, but he blurred again before the magic touched him.

"You're finished, Aedth," a harsh voice declared. "Turn around and face your end like a man."

He felt his spies converging on them, their daggers ready, and his own hatred swelling. "You cannae end me, idiot. I'm no' a man anymore." He wanted to watch this, at least for a moment, and swung around to see Broden and his wench advancing on him. "Soon I'll become the prince of demons."

The female made a rude sound. "They already have one."

Galan's spies rushed out of the trees toward the pair, their blades glittering in the sunlight. They lunged at the trapper and the mortal slut, slashing and stabbing. To Galan's surprise the female fought just as fiercely as Broden to repel their attackers.

He'd hoped to preserve some of his spies, but it soon became clear he'd have to sacrifice them all. Sending out the final command, he smiled as they grew frenzied, no longer trying to protect themselves from injury. Blood darkened the earth all around them by the time the rest of the Mag Raith reached them.

Knowing he'd ended at least two of the wretched clan, and the others would be kept busy long enough to allow his escape, Galan laughed and ran deeper into the forest.

Chapter Twenty-Eight

THE THRESH OF bodies and the pain of her wounds didn't stop Mariena from fighting for her life. Dozens of blank-faced people, most thin and emaciated, slashed at her over and over. She felt Broden's back against hers as he fought from the other side, but soon there were simply too many.

"Mag Raith *gu bráth*," Domnall shouted as he charged into the mass of hacking, slashing attackers, followed by Mael and Kiaran.

Arrows flew all around Mariena, and beyond the crush she caught a glimpse of Edane shooting into the mass of bodies. Somehow he only hit the attackers, who began falling to the ground. The others simply climbed on top of them and hacked at her and Broden.

A blade sliced into her neck before the wasted man wielding it staggered back and fell, his head rolling from his body.

The roar of the clan's voices added to the rush in Mariena's ears as she fell to her knees, and felt Broden turn and cover her with his body, pressing her to the ground. He jerked atop her as more of their attackers began to fall around them. Only when her lover's weight disappeared did Mariena understand that it was over.

Domnall gently turned her onto her side, and clapped his hand over a wound in her neck. "Edane, to me."

Mariena turned her head and saw Broden on the ground beside her. Blood covered his face and soaked his hair, and countless wounds riddled his body. She knew he was dead when Edane looked at him and then Domnall and shook his head. Her own heart seemed to be beating only now and then, and she could feel a terrible coldness seeping from her limbs into her body. She sensed she had only a few moments left to act.

She could not cheat death as the other women had, but she still had a chance to see that Broden would.

"No, *mon ami*," she whispered when the chieftain tried to lift her. "Put me in his arms. That is where I wish to die."

Domnall eyed Edane, who nodded, and then shifted her over, gently placing her atop her lover.

Mariena felt her power flash through her the moment her flesh touched Broden's. The pain of his wounds followed, slicing into her from every side as her flesh absorbed them. She used the last of her will to move her head so that her cheek covered his heart. When she felt it throb again, she felt her own stutter.

Strange thoughts moved through her mind. The mission she'd thought the demon had given her had actually been her last assignment for the resistance, to assassinate the Butcher of Lyon. Somehow the memory of that grim failure from her time had become entangled with what the traitor had wished her to do at Dun Chaill, which only now she remembered.

You must find my brother Culvar, and tell him I live. When the time is right I shall come. Together we shall end the Sluath.

Although she had failed the demon, she had saved the man she loved. Broden would live. She could go to her rest now, and take that victory with her.

Mariena closed her eyes and at last surrendered.

Chapter Twenty-Nine

BRODEN AWOKE IN the white chamber where the Sluath had kept him imprisoned. Although now it stood empty, he remembered when Seabhag first dragged her into the chamber.

Broden had kept his distance and spoken to her as softly as he could manage, explaining what had happened to her. She'd said nothing but kept to the other side of the chamber, arming herself and watching him with hatred in her eyes. It was only when he'd turned his back for a moment to fetch the coverlet from the bed that she'd spoken.

"They whipped you," she said, her accent making the words sound almost like a caress. "You are not one of them."

"No, lass. I'm mortal and a slave, like ye." He

was glad he still bled a little, for his face offered no reassurance. “They’ve punished me many times since I came here with my brothers.”

Slowly she put down the pitcher. Her blue-gold eyes shifted as she took a cloth from the eating table and used it to wipe her face. Beneath the thick clay her skin looked as white as snow. “Where are these brothers?”

“Somewhere here,” he said. “I see them at times, but I dinnae ken where they’re kept now.”

“Then we must find them.” She went to the fountain to splash her face, and then dried it with the hem of her drab gown. Damp spikes of her pale hair framed her strong, lovely features as she came to him, and held out her hand. “My name is Mariena Douet.”

In that moment they had become allies, bonding as closely as Broden had with his Mag Raith brothers. She asked many questions that he tried to answer, but too much about the underworld still bewildered him. He tried to explain how time moved differently here with no day or night. He had learned to count the hours by his morning and evening meals. The Sluath did not always feed him, however, so it remained an imperfect method.

She spent her first hour with him pacing around the chamber, examining every feature closely. "How do we escape?"

"I cannae tell ye, my lady," he admitted. "'Tis no entry or windows but those the demons make and unmake. As they move me I've tried to run, yet they ever catch me in the tunnels. I've fought the guards, but they're stronger and faster, and too many."

"Like the Nazis," Mariena muttered, and gave him a measuring look. "Very well, *mon ami.* We will have to outsmart them."

His prison chamber suddenly darkened around him, and Broden found himself back in his broch at the Mag Raith settlement. Sileas stood watching him, the sneer on her face faltering as he looked back at her.

"From this ye cannae flee," his sire's mate told him, as she had innumerable times in his memories.

This time he would not hold his tongue. "My *máthair* died at my birth. I left the tribe. You had my sire and your son to give you comfort. Why wasnae that enough for you?"

"He loved her," Sileas told him. "A filthy bed slave—and ye her image."

Jealousy over a woman long dead, who had not even chosen to bed his sire. Broden had always feared Sileas, but now he saw how small and petty she was.

"Ye broke the truce when ye disappeared. The Carrack attacked again, and killed my son." Her face began to wrinkle and turn ashen. What little beauty she possessed faded as she shriveled and her back bowed. "The tribe cast me out. The Mag Raith vanished soon after ye. I ended a beggar with naught."

As the shadows swallowed her, Sileas looked much like the demons after they died. But only when her withered face disappeared did Broden finally take in her words.

My vanishing tortured her far more than the Carrack ever could. She never learned my fate, nor took her vengeance on me.

A blaze of warmth flooded through him, erasing the chill that had been spreading. It felt of Mariena, and he sighed with pleasure. She had found him again, and now nothing would ever part them.

Above Broden a blue sky stretched, framed along the edges by Dun Chaill's ancient walls and the green bounty of the trees. He felt the vague ache of his body as he recalled the chaos during the attack of Galan's mortals in the forest.

"Mariena." The only reason he drew breath had to be her.

Broden struggled upright, and turned until he saw his lady, partly wrapped in his tartan, now blood-soaked. Every muscle in his body protested as he got to his feet and staggered over to her. When he saw the wounds that had nearly dismembered her body he fell to his knees. Gently he pressed his fingers to her throat, but felt no pulse there.

She hadn't simply healed him. Rage rose in his chest as understanding dawned. She'd taken his place in death.

"*No*," he bellowed to the sky in his wretched voice.

A faint echo of it returned from the keepe's walls before fading into the forest.

No, he mouthed soundlessly, over and over as he collapsed beside his dead lover. His vision dimmed as if he were going blind again. She'd told him that the Sluath ink was what had awakened the clan's women from death, but hers had been damaged. She must have known that when she died she would not attain immortality as the other women had.

"You said you loved me," he told her. "You must heal yourself now, and return to me, my lady." When she didn't move he cradled her face between his shaking hands. "You shall do this for me. I command you now."

"Her power only heals others," a low, grating voice said.

A strangely-shaped shadow stretched over Mariena. Before Broden could react a dark blue light enveloped him, slamming him back to the ground. Even using his strength, he couldn't break free. He looked up and the blood froze in his veins. Standing above him was the thing Nellie had described, the crippled, disfigured wretch that had built Dun Chaill and had tormented them all with its traps and schemes. She had called it a monster, and the villagers of Wachvale the *kithan*.

The watcher.

He had the features and body of a very large human male, but also resembled the prince of the Sluath, had that fack been taken apart and put back together wrongly. He had a crooked arm and a badly crippled leg, and leaned heavily on a thick tree branch used as a crutch. A scent like that of the darker places in the forest came from his shabby garments, thick and pervasive. Yet while his eyes had the same yellow cast as the demon prince's, they looked oddly human as he gazed down at Mariena.

Only now did Broden realize that the clan had vanished to chase after Galan. He was alone with the creature.

"Release me and I'll amuse you, demon," he told it through clenched teeth. He fought the magic pinning him down. "She's dead. You cannae harm her."

"I did that when I blinded you, Pritani," the watcher said in a voice that sounded as rasping and ruined as Broden's. With difficulty he lowered himself to her other side, and pulled back the tartan from her breast. "I must make amends now."

Broden swore as the watcher tore open her bodice, and slapped his hand over her shoulder. "Leave her alone, you perverse bastart."

"My name is Culvar," the demon told him, sounding almost reproving. "Dun Chaill is my home. Now shut up so I can concentrate."

When he swore at him again Culvar flicked

his free hand, and a band of indigo light sealed Broden's mouth.

The watcher closed his eyes and murmured, and more dark blue light glowed around the hand he held to Mariena's shoulder. When he lifted it away the light rolled over the gash in her flesh, closing the wound. Once the skin had grown smooth again the magic traced along the glyphs, filling in the ink that had been damaged. The silvery tattoo took on a bright golden hue.

Broden stared at the gleaming ink until Culvar took hold of her hand and pressed it against his crippled leg. The demon was trying to force Mariena to heal him, and Broden would have torn himself in two to stop that. He strained against the magic, only managing to jerk his body back and forth.

Yet after a long moment Culvar shook his head and released her hand.

"I've restored her skinwork," he told Broden. "Your lady will have that which my sister gave to her." He used the stick to rise upright, swaying a little before he regained his balance. He looked upon Mariena again, his expression almost wistful now. "Tell the healer that Culvar keeps his promises."

The magic holding Broden down vanished, and he shoved himself to his feet as Culvar hobbled back toward the stronghold. He would have pursued him, but a soft sound made him look down at his dead lover.

Mariena's chest rose and fell as she began breathing, and the wounds on her body shrank and closed. Her lips parted as she murmured something, and then her eyelashes fluttered.

Broden dropped down beside her, taking her hands in his as she slowly roused and looked up at him. But in the next instant, her eyes darted to the surrounding trees.

"Galan escaped," he told her, "but the clan pursues him." As her gaze met his, it softened but then turned puzzled. "The watcher came to repair your ink and bring you back to me." He felt his own gaze grow hard. "Gods, Mariena, you took my death from me. How could you–"

"Pah. I was dying, and I love you, and this I could give to you. Your gods would agree with me. Your heart, it is not so black as mine. Your hair is prettier." She touched his arm. "So is your tattoo."

Glancing at the now-golden glyphs gleaming

on his flesh, Broden shook his head. "I can give you naught but myself."

"You are all I want." Mariena wrinkled her nose. "And a very long bath." The sound of shocked shouts made her look over toward the forest. "Our clan returns."

Domnall reached them first, his expression grim. "Galan escaped. I've sent Edane and Kiaran and Mael to ride patrol, but 'tis likely he's gone back to the Sluath."

"How are you two breathing?" Jenna demanded as she reached them. "You were both dead when we left, and you're outside the castle."

"It is the long story, *ma copine*." Mariena patted her hand. "We must talk about that and many things."

"Aye, but later," Broden said as he helped his lover up from the ground. "Now we sorely need a bath." He met Rosealise's astonished gaze. "We found the millhouse."

"It grinds people," Mariena told her. "But not anymore."

"Indeed." The housekeeper pursed her lips as she glanced at the stronghold. "Well, then I think I would rather have another quern."

Chapter Thirty

GALAN KEPT WATCH until he saw all of the Mag Raith return to the castle and disappear inside. Domnall emerged soon after that, and rode out on a horse to patrol the barrier. After several hours Mael took his place. The kestrels performed their own flying patrol over the stronghold, and he saw the silhouette of a third hunter, likely Kiaran, standing watch in one of the towers.

They believed they could protect themselves, with only nine to defend this Dun Chaill—and four of them wenches—against him, and perhaps they could. But once the demon hordes descended on them, they would know defeat and death at last.

With Galan leading that legion himself, no keepe could withstand them.

Ascending into the trees and cloaking himself had been a canny move, for the clan had rushed beneath him without ever realizing he hadn't left the forest. That had allowed Galan to witness Culvar limping out of the stronghold to resurrect Broden's dead lover. It had fascinated him to see the magic he used to repair the wench's Sluath slave tattoo. He had thought the glyphs simply marked slaves as property, but from the healing the female had experienced it seemed they contained significant power.

Using such tattoos might even be the means by which Culvar resurrected mortals.

He had to find out more about the magic of the Sluath glyphs before he made another attempt to capture Culvar. If all went as he planned, he would enjoy the same powers and immortality as the hunters possessed before he took the throne from Iolar.

Once he ruled the demons, Galan would have all the power and might he needed to settle other matters with the Moss Dapple and Bhaltair Flen. He might even hunt Ruadri, the son he'd always despised, and see what it took to kill a Pritani made immortal by druids.

Fiana loved him more. Of that he was certain now. That's why she was smiling as she birthed him. She treasured that overlarge brat more than the husband who adored her.

When Mael rode to the far side of the castle on his next pass, Galan descended from the tree and made his way through the forest toward the opposite side. As he passed through the barrier, he tripped over the corpse of the dead weakling he'd throttled and left to rot. Insects now swarmed the remains, the limbs of which looked as if they'd been gnawed on in places by larger predators.

For a moment the dead mortal's face shimmered, and turned into Fiana's blank-eyed stare.

Galan licked his lips and looked out toward the distant lights on the horizon. Yes, he had much to do this night.

Chapter Thirty-One

DEEP BENEATH DUN Chaill Cul hobbled through his tunnels as he made his way to his spell chamber. Mariena should have healed him, but the moment he'd pressed her hand against his leg he felt no relief. It only took another moment to realize why she couldn't help him. None of his injuries were new.

She was a healer. Everything wrong with him had already healed.

At least saving her from death had not required him to use his resurrection power, which he had been prepared to do. Instead, repairing the tattoo on her shoulder had restored its magic, which then took care of the rest. Like the other females she had immortality now.

He went to his potions cabinet, and took out a powerful pain killer. He drank the entire bottle, grimacing as it burned its way through his half-Sluath flesh to curdle in his belly. The Pritani potions only worked to blunt his pain instead of removing it. Still, a half-measure of ease was better than nothing.

He eased his bulk down on the ritual platform where he had spent decades studying the scrolls and tablets he'd carefully preserved over the centuries. Most belonged to a single shaman who had come to Dun Chaill in search of his missing acolyte. Although Cul had always killed every mortal who drew too near to the stronghold, he'd quickly realized the old man's value. An expert in Pritani magic, the shaman also had more power than any mortal he'd ever encountered.

After being captured and imprisoned in Cul's lair, the shaman had offered to teach him everything he had yet to master. This in exchange for what he most wanted, and it wasn't his missing acolyte.

Cul had agreed. It wasn't as if anyone could make him hold up his part of the bargain, but in the end he had done that, too.

The potion finally began to spread some relief

through Cul's limbs, and he rose again to limp out of the chamber. Now that Galan knew the location of Dun Chaill, and the fact that it protected the Mag Raith, the Sluath would be coming—just as Cul had planned since the day the intruders had arrived.

It was time to finish this, which meant beginning his final preparations.

Two iron warriors came into the passage, marching up to him before stopping and awaiting his command.

"Open the caches in the casement," Cul told them as he leaned on his crutch. "Once you've released all the warriors, bring the old shaman to my spell chamber."

Chapter Thirty-Two

MARIENA SOAKED HAPPILY in the heated waters of the bathing chamber as she watched Broden standing in a big wash tub. His muscles flexed as he scrubbed the last of the blood and grime from his tall, perfect body. He'd first done the same for her, and they'd discovered that her awakening to immortality had erased every wound and scar on her body. She had become as perfect as a newborn, which was exactly how she felt.

To see him alive and breathing and healed was her only wish. She would never have to dream again.

When Broden told her what the watcher had done, Mariena felt just as confused as he did. Why he had saved her when he had killed so many didn't make sense to her, which seemed even odder.

She had been a killer, too.

The grimness of Mariena's life before being captured by the Sluath might always blacken her heart. She had assassinated many evil men for the Alliance, but with her memories returned she understood why she didn't regret it. Her actions had been no different than any soldier's. She had simply fought in the shadows instead of on the battlefields. But she didn't have to be an assassin any more. She had only to be with Broden, and fight with the clan to protect their home.

That battle, she sensed, was looming on the horizon. The Sluath would be coming for them, and soon.

"You are clean enough, *mon charmant*," she told him as she climbed out and lugged a water pail over to him. She stood on her toes and dumped it over his head. "And do not forget, I am naked now, and Kiaran still does not have a woman."

Broden regarded her with a long, silent look. "You were much nicer in the underworld."

He stepped out of the tub, his beautiful body gleaming and clean, and his magnificent shaft rising and swelling for her.

"Oh, but I forget," she said as she stepped back. "We should tell the clan all that happened with this Culvar. There are all the things I have not told them, and I am hungry, too. But not for bread. Pah. I change my mind. Without bread, I would have to stop being French."

He advanced on her.

Mariena held up one hand. "At least tell me you love me before you jump on me and make me your slave again."

Broden's hand caught hers, and he brought it to his lips.

"I adore you. You're the lady of my dreams." His dark eyes filled with emotion as he pressed a kiss against her knuckles. "I dinnae want a slave. I wish to mate with you. You'll be my wife."

"Hmm. I should first tell you that I was an assassin for the resistance in France," she murmured, relishing the touch of his lips. "I killed many Nazis. Quickly. They did not suffer." When he glanced up at her she shrugged. "Well, there was one or two who suffered this much." She pinched the air. "But they were very bad."

"'Tis why I'm safer with you." He glided his mouth over the inside of her wrist, and then tugged her against him. "Say you'll be my wife, and love me forever, *a thasgaidh*."

"Perhaps, if you learn to speak French." She curled her arm around his neck. "First lesson: *je t'aime,* Mariena."

Sneak Peek

Kiaran (Immortal Highlander, Clan Mag Raith Book 5)

Excerpt

CHAPTER ONE

Chapter One

A HEAVY MIST and thin gray skies greeted the new day and Kiaran mag Raith as he walked out of the stronghold. Such damp chill spelled the end of summer in the Scottish highlands, or so he recalled from a time now made equally foggy. He could blame too many centuries and his general disinterest for his fading memories, but that had become a convenient excuse.

"Fair morning, Brother," Broden mag Raith greeted him as he walked out from the barn. The smile on the trapper's handsome face echoed the glowing joy in his eyes. "I'd offer to take morning patrol for you–"

"–but I will hurt him if he does," Mariena Douet said as she joined them. Tall, slender and strong, the pale Frenchwoman also appeared blissful. "Of course, I will feel guilty after and heal him. Absorbing his wounds will then make me suffer, which will hurt him more, and he will–" She broke off in a laugh as Broden scooped her up and tossed her over his shoulder.

"Another time, Brother," the trapper said as he carried his lover toward the stronghold.

"Never fall in love, *mon ami*," Mariena called back to him. "It is the mess."

Of all the things Kiaran might assure her, it was that. "Aye, my lady."

Once they entered the stronghold the falconer didn't bother to continue feigning a smile. Appreciating or even envying the happiness Broden and his lady had found together wasn't impossible for him. It simply required more effort than he cared to make. Since coming to the ruined castle of

Dun Chaill with his band of Pritani brothers, Kiaran had felt himself growing quieter, more detached, and less interested in everything. He'd also done things of which he should have felt ashamed, but truly didn't. The changes had not been entirely unexpected, but they now added to the inescapable burdens he had brought with him.

Soon, Kiaran thought as he rolled his aching shoulders, he would have to act, before he no longer cared about the consequences.

A flutter of black-spotted wings fanned his face before a small, gray-headed kestrel alighted on his shoulder. Sift chittered, his dark eyes catching the first rays of sun and turning a rich golden amber. Through the mind connection Kiaran shared with the raptor he saw a flash of his own strong features, carved stark and cold by weariness. The red-gold mane that framed them looked tangled and wild, but it was the dark blue eyes staring at him from his own thoughts that made him end the link.

He hated seeing the flat lifelessness in them.

Sift pecked at his ear and uttered a scolding sound. Hardly larger than a man's fist, the raptor had been the first male kestrel Kiaran had tamed.

Sift usually wasn't the first to greet him in the morning, however, which stirred his sluggish curiosity.

"Where is your lady and the flight?" Kiaran murmured to the kestrel, who cried sharply before he flew off toward the forest.

Following the bird took less effort than reaching out with his tired mind to locate the rest of the kestrels. Using his power to see through the eyes of his raptors had become more difficult since his nights had grown sleepless and dreary. More often now, when he tried, the images from the birds returned in a nonsensical jumble.

'Tisnae the lack of sleep. You're losing your power. Soon the kestrels shall fly away from you.

Kiaran shoved aside that growing fear as he made his way into the ancient forest. While his raptors meant everything to him, even that worry no longer preyed on him as it had.

At last he saw all the kestrels hovering over a small clearing with a swath of broken, wilting lilies and fern. The flowers and plants had been wrenched out of the ground by some disturbance, and lay heaped over a long narrow mound along with many slender branches from the surrounding trees.

Drawing his sword as he scanned the clearing for signs of intruders, Kiaran called out, "Who comes here? Show yourself."

A low, soft moan came from the lilies, and the kestrels floated down and disappeared beneath the debris.

Quickly he waded into the ruined greenery, halting as he saw what had fallen into the forest. "Fack me."

The female lay on her side, her long hair spilling like spun garnet across her face, shoulders and breasts. Petals from the lilies covered her as if she'd been strewn with them by an adoring lover, and their cool sweet scent enveloped her. The rose-gold tint of her skin and faint shimmering movement of her hair assured him that she was alive. All around her his kestrels nestled as if trying to warm her with their small bodies. Dive, the flight's dominant female, looked up at him with something like despair in her dark eyes.

"'Twill be well," Kiaran said. "Let me see to her." He sheathed his blade and kneeled down as he gently turned her onto her back, scattering the birds.

Her young, strong body had not a mark on it, and appeared to be as well-nourished and cosseted as that of a noble woman. She wore nothing but a loop of thin leather with a gleaming pendant around her throat. Looking over her torso and limbs to check for injuries, of which he saw none, he pulled off his tartan and covered her with it. Only then did he brush the hair back from her mouth and eyes.

She might have the body of a queen, but she had the face of a goddess.

Kiaran slowly took his hand away from her, but he couldn't stop himself from staring. Throughout his long life he'd seen many lovely females, including the four that had mated with his Mag Raith brothers. This lady made all of them pale and vanish from his thoughts.

Was it the pure symmetry of her features that bewitched him? From the elegant wings of her dark red brows to the superb camber of her jaw, she seemed unearthly faultless. Glints of gold tipped her auburn lashes. Her full lips, slightly parted, showed a tiny glimpse of teeth like pearls. Surely she had the most beautiful skin he'd ever beheld. To look upon her was to believe in the Gods again, for no hand but those of the almighty ones could have created such a female.

Blindly Kiaran reached for her hand to hold it between his own. "My lady?"

She didn't stir, and when he glanced down he saw the small black-inked glyphs that covered her right hand from wrist to fingertips. Like him and the rest of the Mag Raith Clan she had been a slave of the Sluath, stolen from her time and taken to their underworld. She must have escaped the demons as they had, with the help of the traitor, and been sent here to be reunited with them.

With me.

Kiaran released her hand to rub his own over his sweating face. All four of the ladies who had found their way back to the Mag Raith had once been lovers with each of his brothers in the underworld. He had been the only one for whom no one had come, which had never greatly concerned him. He'd bedded enough wenches over his long life to satisfy his physical needs, but his heart had never once been stirred by any female. Only now this magnificent lady lay before him, like some boon for a wish he'd never made.

No, she cannae be mine.

Taking hold of the pendant around her neck, Kiaran examined it more closely. It had been fashioned from a carved shell that, like the leather strip, looked very old and worn. He could almost make out a face that had been etched into it, perhaps that of a man. He'd seen similar pendants made by ancient Pritani, usually exchanged and worn by mates. Could she have come from the distant past instead of the future?

How long he knelt there studying her Kiaran didn't know. Only when Dive made a sharp sound did he shake off his bewilderment and try gently to wake her again. She remained limp and still, so he would have to carry her back to the stronghold. His arms shook as he reached for her, and lifted her out of the flowers, bringing with her a heady wave of greenery and lilies.

The kestrels took to their wings and hovered, watching him.

The weight of her felt soft rather than heavy against Kiaran's chest, and when he turned to leave the clearing her face touched his neck. He could feel her lips against his skin as if she were kissing him, and it sent a rush of weakness through his belly and legs. At the same time his blood roared in his ears, and his heart pounded like a war drum. He felt more alive than he had since awakening in the ash grove after escaping the Sluath. She might not be his, but she'd made him hers.

Gods help her.

• • • • •

Buy *Kiaran (Immortal Highlander, Clan Mag Raith Book 5)*

Glossary

Here are some brief definitions to help you navigate the medieval world of the Clan Mag Raith series, and also Mariena's French and German below.

Clan Mag Raith

a thasgaidh: Scots Gaelic for "my darling"
amaro: a bittersweet herbal liqueur blended with gin and vermouth to make a Hanky-Panky cocktail
aquila: Latin for "eagle", the standard of a Roman legion
aulden: medieval slang for "archaic"
bairn: child
Banbury tale: Victorian slang for a nonsensical

story
bannock: a round, flat loaf of unleavened Scottish bread
bloodwort: alternate name for yarrow
bloomers: Victorian word for "trousers"
blue-stocking: Victorian slang for "intellectual"
boak: Scottish slang for "vomit"
borage: alternate name for starflower (*Borago officinalis*)
broch: an ancient round hollow-walled structure found only in Scotland
burraidh: Scots Gaelic for "bully"
cac: Scots gaelic for "shit"
chain hoist: tackle and chain device used to lift heavy objects
chanter: a woodwind instrument used alone as practice for playing the bagpipes
chebs: Scottish slang for "breasts"
conclave: druid ruling body
coopered: Victorian slang for worn out
Cornovii: name by which two, or three, tribes were known in Roman Britain
cossetted: cared for in an overindulgent way
cottar: an agricultural worker or tenant given lodgings in return for work
Cuingealach: Scots Gaelic for "the narrow pass"

curate: a member of the clergy engaged as an assistant to a vicar, rector, or parish priest
deadfall trap: a type of trap fashioned to drop a heavy weight on the prey
deamhan (plural: *deamhanan*): Scots Gaelic for demon
dolabra: Latin for "pickaxe"
don't take any wooden nickels: early 20th century American slang for "don't do something stupid"
doss: leaves, moss, and other detritus covering the ground dru-wid: Proto Celtic word; an early form of "druid"
drystane: a construction of stacked stone or rock that is not mortared together
dunnage: Victorian slang for "clothing"
fash: feel upset or worried
fizzing: Victorian slang for "first-rate" or "excellent"
fletching: feathering an arrow
floorer: Victorian slang for "knocking someone down"
flummery: a custard-like Welsh dessert made from milk, beaten eggs and fruit
footman: a liveried servant whose duties include admitting visitors and waiting at table
forthright: honest

fortitude: courage under pressure
frittata: Italian egg dish similar to a crustless quiche
gainsay: contradict
give the sack: English slang for "firing someone from their job"
gladii: Latin plural of *gladius* or “sword”
glock: Victorian slang for “half-wit”
gongoozler: Victorian slang for "an idle, dawdling person"
goof: early 20th century American slang for "a man in love"
grice: a breed of swine found in the Highlands and Islands of Scotland and in Ireland
groat: a type of medieval silver coin worth approximately four pence
gu bràth: Scots Gaelic for forever, or until Judgment
Guédelon: a 25-year-long archaeological experiment in Treigny, France to recreate a 13th century castle
hold your wheesht: Scottish slang term for "maintaining silence and calm"
hoor: medieval slang for "whore", "prostitute"
Hussar: member of the light cavalry
in the scud: Scottish slang for “naked”
jem: Medieval Scots slang for a person prized for

beauty and excellence, a "gem"
jess: a short leather strap that is fastened around each leg of a hawk
kirk: Scottish slang for "church"
kithan: Medieval Scots term for a "demon"
knacker: Victorian slang for "an old, useless horse"
laudanum: a tincture of opium
luaidh: Scots Gaelic for "loved one" or "darling"
maister: medieval slang for "master" or "leader"
make a stuffed bird laugh: Victorian slang phrase for something that is "preposterous or contemptible"
marster: medieval slang for "master"
máthair: Scots Gaelic for "mother"
Mulligatawny soup: a spicy British soup
nag: slang for horse
naught-man: an unearthly creature that only looks like a man
nock: the slotted end of an arrow that holds it in place on the bowstring
panay: alternate name for self-heal (*Prunella vulgaris*)
pantaloons: Victorian word for "trousers"
parti: the ideas or plans influencing an architect's design

peignoir: Victorian-era woman's garment similar to a "negligee or a light dressing gown"
peridot: a green semi-precious mineral, a variety of olivine
peyrl: Scots Gaelic for "pearl"
plumbata: lead-weighted throwing dart used by the Romans
pomatum: greasy, waxy, or water-based substance used to style hair
quern: a primitive hand mill for grinding grain made of two stones
rollicking: fun and boisterous
rooing: removing sheep's loose fleece by hand-pulling
sham: false, fake
sica: a long curved dagger
skeg: Scots Gaelic for "demon"
sleep-in: Victorian slang for sleeping in late
spend: ejaculate
stand hunt: to watch for prey from a blind or place of concealment
stele: an upright pillar bearing inscriptions
stockman: a person who looks after livestock
strewing: plants scattered on the floor as fragrance, insecticide, and disinfectant
tapachd: Scots Gaelic for "an ability of confident

character not to be afraid or easily intimidated”
taverit: Scottish slang for "worn out, exhausted"
tear bottle: Used in the Victorian revival of the ancient custom of catching tears of mourning in a small vial with a loose stopper. When the bottled tears evaporated, the period of mourning was considered over.
touch-reader: a person with psychometric ability; someone who touch objects to envision their history
trigging: in stonework, using wedge pieces to secure a construct
treadwheel crane: a human-powered wooden wheeled device used for hoisting and lowering materials
trodge: Scottish slang for “trudge”
valise: a small traveling bag or suitcase
woundwort: alternate name for wound healer (*Anthyllis vulneraria*)
yelm: bundled block of straw or grasses used in thatching

French to English:

bien sûr: of course
boche: blockhead, a derogatory term used during

WWII for Nazi soldiers
bon sang: damn it
bonjour: good morning
bravo: well done
calme-toi: calm down
c'est bon: French for "it's good"
coup d'un soir: one-night stand
désolé: I'm sorry (casual form)
enchanté: nice to meet you
Favor: the name of a WWII-era French bicycle manufacturer
hostilité: hostility
imbécile: imbecile, stupid
je me suis échappé: I escaped
je suis le cygne: I am the swan
je t'aime: I love you
la patronne: the boss
le cygne: the swan
ma chére amie: my dear friend
ma copine: my friend
mademoiselle: French for "Miss"
merde alors: shit then
mon ami: my friend
mon ange: my angel
mon charmant: my charming one
mon couer: my heart

mon cygne: my swan
mon dieu: my god
monsieur: sir
n'aie pas peur: French for """Don't be afraid"
ne pleure pas: I am not crying
non: French for "no"
*nous sommes tes ami*s: French for "We are your friends"
oui: French for "yes"
putain: whore
resistants: resisters, a slang term for WWII French Resistance agents
reste en arriére: French for "Stay back"
trés bon: very good
vous parlez anglaise: French for "Do you speak English?"

German to English:

fuhrer: leader
Gestapo: secret state police (formally Geheime Staatspolizei)
guten abend, herren: good evening, gentlemen
Hauptsturmführer: Nazi party paramilitary rank, equal to Captain in the German army
Luftwaffe: Air Force

Pronunciation Guide

A selection of the more challenging words in the Immortal Highlander, Clan Mag Raith series. French and German follow below.

a thasgaidh: AH-tas-GEH
Aklen: ACK-lin
aquila: uh-KEE-lah
Bacchanalian: back-NIL-ee-ahn
bannock: BAN-ick
boak: BOWK
Bridget McMurphy: BRIH-jet mick-MER-fee
Broden mag Raith: BRO-din MAG RAYTH
burraidh: BURR-ee
cac: kak
Carac: CARE-ick
Clamhan: CLEM-en

Clarinda Gowdon: kler-IN-dah GOW-don
Cornovii: core-KNOW-vee-eye
Cuingealach: kwin-GILL-ock
Cul: CULL
Danar: dah-NAH
Dapper: DAH-purr
Darro: DAR-oh
deamhan: DEE-man
dolabra: dohl-AH-brah
Domnall mag Raith: DOM-nall MAG RAYTH
Druman: DREW-mawn
Dun Chaill: DOON CHAYLE
Eara: EER-ah
Edane mag Raith: eh-DAYN MAG RAYTH
Fargas: FAR-gus
Fiana: FEYE-eh-nah
Fraser: FRAY-zir
Frew: FREE
frittata: free-TAH-tah
Galan Aedth: gal-AHN EEDTH
gladii: GLAHD-ee-ee
groat: GROWT
gu bràth: GOO BRATH
Hal Maxwell: HOWL MACK-swell
Helen Frances Quinn: HELL-uhn
FRAN-sess KWIN

Hussar: hoo-ZAHR
Iolar: EYE-el-er
Jackie Facelli: JA-kee fah-CHELL-ee
Jaeg: YEGG
jem: GEM
Jenna Cameron: JEHN-nah CAM-er-ahn
John McMurphy: JAWN mick-MER-fee
Josef: HOE-zef
Kehl: HEEL
Kiaran mag Raith: KEER-ahn MAG RAYTH
kithan: KEY-tin
laudanum: LAH-deh-num
luaidh: LOO-ee
Lyle Gordon: lie-EL GORE-din
Mael mag Raith: MAIL MAG RAYTH
maister: MAY-ster
Marie-Anne: mah-REE-en
Mariena Douet: mah-REE-nah DOO-eh
marster: MAR-stir
Mary Gowdon: MARE-ee GOW-don
máthair: muh-THERE
Meirneal: MEER-nee-el
Michael Patrick Quinn: MYK-uhl
PAH-treek KWIN
Mickie: MIH-kee
Mulligatawny: mull-eh-gah-TAWN-ee

Nectan: NECK-tin
Nellie: NELL-ee
parti: PAR-tee
peignoir: pen-WAH
peyrl: PEH-rill
plumbata: PLOOM-bah-tah
pomatum: pah-MADE-uhm
quern: KWERN
Rodney Percell: RAHD-knee purr-SELL
Rosealise Dashlock: roh-see-AH-less DASH-lock
Seabhag: SHAH-vock
Serca: SAIR-eh-kah
sica: SEE-kah
Sileas: SIGH-lee-ess
skeg: SKEHG
Sluath: SLEW-ahth
tapachd: TAH-peed
taverit: tah-VAIR-eet
tisane: TEE-zahn
trodge: TRAHJ
valise: vuh-LEES
Wachvale: WATCH-veil
wheesht: WEESHT

French words:

bien sûr: BEE-yen SIR
boche: BOSH
bon sang: BOW SAW
bonjour: bah-ZHURE
bravo: BRA-voh
calme-toi: CAL-meh TWAH
coup d'un soir: COO-der SWAH
désolé: DEZ-oh-lay
enchanté: aw-shawn-TAY
hostilité: hoe-STILL-lee-tay
imbécile: eyem-bee-SILL-lay
je me suis échappé: ZHAY MAY SWEE eh-SHAH-pay
je suis le cygne: ZHUH SWEE -LAH-SEEN
je t'aime: zhuh TEM
la patronne: LAH PAH-tren
le cygne: LUH SEEN
Lyon: lee-AWN
ma chére amie: MAH SHER ah-MEE
ma copine: MAH coh-PEEN
merde alors: MARED a-LOR
mon ami: MAWN ah-MEE
mon ange: MAWN ANZH
mon charmant: MAWN shar-MAWN
mon couer: MAWN CUR
mon cygne: MAWN SEEN

mon dieu: MAWN DEW
monsieur: meh-SYOUR
ne pleure pas: NEH PLUR PAH
putain: pooh-TAWN
resistants: ray-ZIS-tawns
trés bon: TRAY BAWN

German words:

fuhrer: FYER-er
Gestapo: gesh-STAH-poh
guten abend, herren: GOO-ten AH-bend HAIR-en
Hauptsturmführer: HAWP-SHTERM-FYER-er
Luftwaffe: LOOFT-wah-fah

Dedication

For Mr. H.

Copyright

Lightning Source UK Ltd.
Milton Keynes UK
UKHW020642060421
381519UK00012B/1025

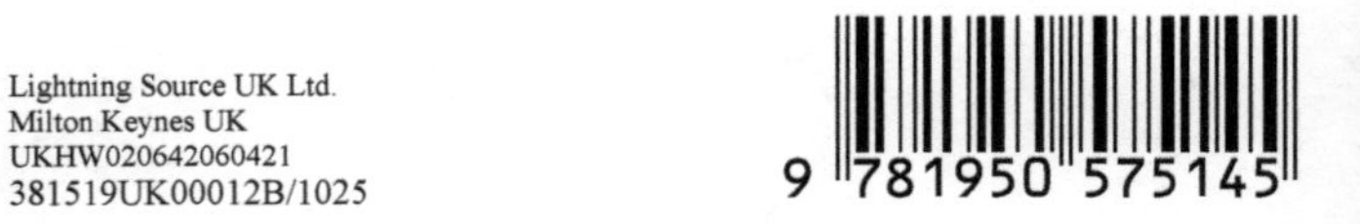